SAGE, ROSEMARY, AND TIME

SAGE, ROSEMARY, AND TIME

A Magical Bookshop Novella

HARMKE BUURSMA

Illusive Press

ISBN 978-1-962506-95-3 (ebook)
ISBN 978-1-962506-96-0 (paperback)

Edited by Megan Sanders
Author photo by Patterson Photography
Cover design by Getcovers.com

Published by Illusive Press
info@illusivepress.com
www.illusivepress.com

For more information about Harmke Buursma and her books, visit www.harmkebuursma.com

First Edition, 2023

For everyone who has ever supported me in making my dream a reality.

Contents

"If one dream should fall and break into a thousand pieces, never be afraid to pick one of those pieces up and begin again."
-Flavia Weedn

I

A Scholarship

"Rosemary, come here," my mother called from the living room, her voice strained yet filled with anticipation. "Look what just arrived."

I dropped the magazine I was reading on top of my bed and rushed down the stairs. As I entered the room, the smell of cigarette smoke mingled with the sound of the television blaring in the background.

A disembodied voice droned from the deep black-and-white television, transposed over footage of soldiers in combat.

"We are only halfway through 1967 and the Vietnam War has already been marked by intense fighting and critical turning points. US forces, alongside South Vietnamese troops, have been engaged in a protracted struggle against the communist Viet Cong and North Vietnamese Army. Let's take a closer look at some of the key developments this year."

My mother sat on the couch, coughing and waving a letter in the air in one hand while the other held out her preferred brand of cigarette, Virginia Slims.

I glanced out the window and saw the mailman walking away from our front yard, his bag now empty. My heart raced with anticipation. Could it be a response from one of the colleges I had applied to? With an eager step, I approached my mother, nervousness growing in my chest. I had applied to a few; I had never been one to put all my eggs into one basket. But if I had to be honest, there was only one choice for me.

"Is it from the Curtis Institute of Music?"

My mother nodded, taking a final drag from her cigarette before pressing it out in the ashtray on the side table. She reached for the letter opener and slit open the envelope.

The television continued to play.

"Back home, the anti-war movement gains momentum as thousands take to the streets, demanding an end to American involvement in Vietnam."

But my attention was focused on the letter my mother held in her hands. I fidgeted with the buttons on my blouse. "I'm too nervous to read it, Mom. Can you do it for me?"

My mother flashed an understanding smile, a bit of mirth sparkling in her gaze. She turned the TV off, a soft hiss exuding from the screen as it turned black.

"Of course, sweetheart." She licked her fingers and unfolded the neatly pressed letter. Her eyes flitted across the paper, and after clearing her throat, she started to read.

Dear Rosemary Scott,

I am delighted to inform you that you have been selected as a recipient of a full scholarship at the Curtis Institute of Music for the upcoming academic year.

"I got in?" I became aware that my hands were trembling. Mother paused, a smile creeping across her face. "Rosemary, you did it. You got accepted." She pushed the letter towards me. "Here, you finish reading it."

I nodded, my heart drumming against my ribcage.

On behalf of the admissions committee and the entire faculty, I extend my warmest congratulations to you.

Your exceptional musical talent and dedication to your craft have truly impressed us. We believe that you possess the potential to make a significant contribution to the world of music, and we are thrilled to offer you this opportunity to further develop your skills and nurture your artistic growth at Curtis.

At the Curtis Institute of Music, you will be joining a prestigious institution renowned for its commitment to excellence in musical education. Our esteemed faculty members are internationally recognized musicians and educators who are dedicated to helping you achieve your highest artistic aspirations. The curriculum at Curtis is designed to provide you with a comprehensive musical education that combines rigorous training, performance opportunities, and a supportive community of fellow musicians.

A surge of exhilaration coursed through my veins, and I couldn't contain my excitement any longer. I grabbed my mother by the arms, lifting her from the blue pin-tucked couch, and together we jumped.

As we jumped, the front door opened and my brother Lyle walked into the room, a backpack slung across his shoulders, and wearing overalls stained from working at the automotive factory. Confusion clouded his face.

"What's all this about?"

Breathless and beaming, I turned to him. "I got accepted into the Curtis Institute of Music."

Lyle's eyes widened, and a smile tugged at his lips. "Congratulations, Rosemary. I knew you could do it. They would be fools not to accept you."

I dropped my mother's hands and pulled my brother in for a hug, careful not to touch the oily stains on his front. "They gave me a full scholarship."

As my mother caught her breath, a hint of a wheeze still present in her cough, she spoke up, "I'm so proud of you, Rosemary. I never doubted for a moment that you would get in."

"All right, all right, that is enough hugging." Lyle patted my shoulder and peeled my arms away from him. "I am in terrible need of a shower."

I pinched my nose and stuck out my tongue at Lyle. "You do smell."

"Very funny." Lyle shook his head and dropped his backpack next to the coat rack.

Mother chuckled. "How about this; Lyle, you go freshen up while Rosemary heads out to give Mrs. Johnson the good news. Then I can prepare something sweet for after dinner since we are celebrating."

"Fudge cake?" I asked hopefully. It was one of my favorite treats, usually only reserved for birthdays.

Mother glanced at the clock above the TV, lips pursing as she did her calculations. "I should have enough time before dinner is ready."

"Yes, thank you, thank you!" I blew my mom a kiss then snatched my shoes from the entryway, hopping between feet as I pulled them on. "I will be right back."

"Give my thanks to Mrs. Johnson," Mother shouted after me as I hurried out the door.

"Will do, Mom."

I hopped on my bicycle, feeling the hot breeze against my face as I pedaled down the familiar streets of my town. The sunlight streamed through the fanned leaves of the towering palm trees, casting dappled shadows on the pavement below.

As I approached Mrs. Johnson's house, I noticed a fellow student stepping out, the front door still ajar. Mrs. Johnson must have spotted me, for she appeared in the doorway, her eyes twinkling as she crossed her arms.

"Rosemary, my dear, did you forget an appointment?" There was a note of concern in her voice. "I didn't think we had a lesson scheduled for today."

I shook my head, a wide grin spreading across my face. "No, Mrs. Johnson, there's no appointment. I just wanted to stop by and share some incredible news with you."

Her brow raised as I dismounted my bicycle and propped it against the white picket fence. Mrs. Johnson beckoned me inside, and I followed her into the cozy living room, the scent of sweet tea lingering in the air.

"What's this news, my dear?" Mrs. Johnson asked, glancing at me.

I took a deep breath, excitement bubbling in my stomach. "I've been accepted into the Curtis Institute of Music."

Mrs. Johnson's eyes widened, and a gasp escaped her lips. "Rosemary, that's wonderful!" Her voice was filled with pride. "I knew you had it in you, my dear."

Tears shimmered in the corners of my eyes as I looked at the woman who had guided me since I was a little girl through hours of piano practice and hand positions. "I couldn't have done it without you, Mrs. Johnson. Your guidance, patience, and belief in me have been invaluable."

A soft smile graced Mrs. Johnson's face, and she reached out to clasp my hands. "You've always been special, Rosemary." Her gaze turned distant, and her voice filled with warmth. "I remember when you were just ten years old, practicing tirelessly, determined to hit every note. Your dedication has always impressed me."

Memories of long hours spent at the piano flooded my mind, and I felt a surge of gratitude for the lessons and the bond we had shared. Mrs. Johnson had been more than just a teacher; she had become a mentor and a friend. And now, because of her, I would be heading to Philadelphia.

"You're my best student, Rosemary," Mrs. Johnson continued, her voice filled with pride. "And I couldn't be happier that you have this opportunity to use and expand your gift at college."

We sat there for a while, reminiscing about the journey

that had led us to this moment. The afternoon sun cast a warm glow over us, and in the presence of my beloved teacher, I felt a deep sense of determination and gratitude.

As I bid Mrs. Johnson farewell and mounted my bicycle once again, I carried her words with me, a guiding light illuminating my path. With the acceptance letter tucked safely in my pocket, I rode back home, where my mother and brother would be waiting for me.

Soon enough, I sat at the kitchen table, savoring the last few bites of my mother's meatloaf. The comforting aroma filled the air, reminding me of countless family dinners over the years. The taste was familiar and comforting, a testament to my mother's love and care. I sighed, feeling the warmth of the meal spread through my body.

As I wiped my mouth with a napkin, my mother rose from her seat and disappeared into the kitchen. I watched with anticipation as she reappeared, carrying her homemade fudge cake on a floral plate. My eyes lit up, and a smile tugged at the corners of my lips. Fudge cake was my absolute favorite.

Placing the cake in the center of the table, my mother grabbed a knife and began to slice it, each piece landing on a waiting plate with precision. My older brother, Lyle, shifted in his seat beside me, his eyes fixed on the mouthwatering dessert.

With the plates of fudge cake now in front of us, we each took a forkful and savored the rich, velvety sweetness. The chocolate melted on my tongue, a decadent indulgence that made my taste buds dance with delight.

Around me, the sound of my family's contented murmurs filled the kitchen. Lyle grinned, licking the last of the frosting from his fork, and my mother's eyes twinkled with affection. At that moment, I couldn't help but feel an overwhelming sense of happiness, a warmth that enveloped me from within.

A deep appreciation swelled in my heart as I glanced at my family. Here they were, supporting me in all my dreams and aspirations. They had been there for every recital, every late-night practice session, and every setback I had encountered along the way ever since father passed away when I was five.

I took another bite of the fudge cake. The future lay ahead, full of promise and possibilities. The acceptance into the Curtis Institute of Music was just the beginning, the stepping stone to a world of melodies and harmonies waiting to be explored.

I couldn't imagine being happier.

As I savored the last crumbs of the fudge cake, I held onto this moment, etching it into the deepest recesses of my heart.

With a soft smile, I whispered to myself, "This is happiness."

2

An Errand

The next day, as the sun cast its golden rays across our small town, the mailman arrived once again, carrying news that wouldn't bring the same joy as the previous day. My heart sank as I watched Lyle's hands tremble, his grip tight on the envelope he clutched. The distinctive emblem of the Selective Service System stamped on it felt like a heavy weight on the otherwise thin letter.

Lyle's voice quivered as he spoke, his words laced with fear and resignation. "Rosemary, I've been selected to report for a physical examination." His voice wavered, and he cleared his throat. We all knew what receiving a draft notice meant. Many men from our town, our neighbors, and our friends, had already been selected and sent to fight overseas.

I reached out, placing a comforting hand on his shoulder. "Maybe there's still a chance they'll disqualify you." I tried to infuse hope into my words. "They can't take everyone."

Lyle's response was laced with a bitter truth. "I'm of good, healthy, American stock, Rosemary." His voice was tinged with sadness. "There's nothing physically wrong with me. Look at how many men from our town have already been called away to fight. I doubt they'll pass me over."

His words hung in the air, heavy with the reality of the situation. The draft had cast its net far and wide, and now it had ensnared my brother, threatening to tear him away from the life he knew. The weight of the situation settled upon us like a suffocating fog.

***

A few weeks passed, and the days blurred together as our town bid farewell to more of its young men, sending them off to unknown fates. Lyle, too, prepared himself for the inevitable. He packed his belongings, his steps heavy.

As he stood by the bus stop, ready to ride out and begin his basic training, I stood beside him, my eyes brimming with tears that threatened to spill over. We exchanged a solemn gaze, a silent understanding passing between us.

Time stood still; the world hushed as we confronted the reality of war. With a heavy heart, I watched him drive off into the distance, the bus becoming smaller and smaller until it blended with the horizon. As he disappeared, I whispered a prayer for his safety, for his return.

Panic gripped my heart when I returned home and found my mother slumped over on the kitchen floor, her fragile form trembling. Tears streaked her cheeks, and her labored breaths echoed through the room. Fear coursed through my veins, urging me into action.

Kneeling beside her, I cradled her in my arms, my voice trembling with desperation. "Mom, please, stay calm. I need to go get help. Just hold on, okay?"

Her eyes met mine, and she nodded weakly, struggling to catch her breath. I rose to my feet, my heart pounding against my chest. We did not yet have a phone at home, and time was of the essence. I had to find someone who could call for an ambulance.

With hurried steps, I rushed out of the house, my mind racing. I ran towards our neighbor's home, my fists pounding on their front door. I could hear my voice, frantic and filled with urgency, calling out for help.

The door swung open, revealing Mrs. Thompson, her face etched with concern as she took in my flustered state. "Rosemary, dear, what's happened?"

Struggling to catch my breath, I blurted out the words, my voice trembling with fear. "I need to call an ambulance. It's my mother. She's... she's in trouble."

Mrs. Thompson's eyes widened, and without hesitation, she ushered me inside. Her living room blurred before my eyes as she rushed to pick up the phone, dialing the emergency number. I could hear her voice, steady and composed, as she relayed the details to the operator.

I stood there, feeling a mix of helplessness and gratitude. Mrs. Thompson had always been kind, but at that moment, her compassion and willingness to assist overwhelmed me.

As Mrs. Thompson hung up the phone, she turned to me, her voice gentle yet firm. "Help is on the way, Rosemary." She rested her hand on my shoulder. "Stay strong, my dear. Your mother will be taken care of."

Together, we waited, each passing second feeling like an eternity. As the distant wail of sirens grew louder, a surge of hope washed over me. Help was coming, and though the future remained uncertain, I clung to the belief that my mother would receive the care she needed. That she would be all right.

And as the ambulance arrived, its flashing lights illuminating the darkening sky, I whispered a silent prayer to whoever was out there listening.

My heart felt heavy as I sat beside my mother in the ambulance, the rhythmic hum of the vehicle punctuating the tense silence. Fear and uncertainty hung in the air, suffocating me as we embarked on this daunting journey.

Minutes later, we arrived at the hospital, and a whirlwind of activity surrounded us. Medical professionals whisked my mother away, promising to take good care of her. I clung to those words, seeking solace in the hope they offered.

Hours dragged by, each passing minute amplifying my anxiety. Finally, the doctor returned to my mother's hospital room, a solemn expression etched on his face. I held my breath, my hands clasped in my lap, awaiting his words.

He pulled up a chair, his eyes filled with empathy, and began to speak. "I've reviewed the x-ray images, and I'm afraid the results are not what we had hoped for." His voice was gentle but tinged with sadness. "Your mother has stage three lung cancer."

The room spun around me as his words settled in. Cancer. The mere mention of the word sent a chill down my spine, filling me with terror and despair. I glanced at my mother, her face pale, her eyes reflecting the shock that mirrored my own.

The doctor continued, explaining the treatment plan that lay ahead. "We will need to start chemotherapy immediately. It's a challenging road, but with the right treatment, there is hope."

Tears welled up in my eyes as I listened, my mind struggling to comprehend the magnitude of what lay before us. I reached out, grasping my mother's hand, offering whatever comfort I could though my mind overflowed with troubling thoughts.

How could it be that only two weeks ago my life had been the happiest it could ever be? Newly graduated from high school, accepted into the Curtis Institute of Music on a full scholarship, and my family together and happily celebrating my achievements. Now, my brother was off to fight in Vietnam. I hadn't been able to listen to the news since, not when it was filled with reports of attacks and men killed. My heart sank. And my mother was ill.

There would be no more going to Philadelphia. I could not leave my mother to deal with doctor visits and chemo treatment by herself. She was going to need me. I felt my dreams of becoming a renowned pianist slipping through my fingers.

Gathering my courage, I turned to the doctor, my voice trembling but resolute. "Thank you for your honesty and for outlining the treatment plan." I grasped my mother's pale hand. "We will fight this together."

The doctor nodded, his gaze filled with compassion. "You're

both strong, and with the support of our medical team, we'll do everything we can to help."

As the doctor left the room, leaving us with the weight of our new reality, I squeezed my mother's hand, vowing to be her pillar of strength. "We'll fight this, Mom. I'll be right by your side every step of the way."

"What about school? You're supposed to leave in a month."

I worried my lip as I gazed at my mother's concerned face. "I can postpone a year; I am certain they'll let me." I knew it was a lie when I said it. The Curtis Institute of Music was highly competitive, and there were very few slots available each year, let alone applicants who received full scholarships. If I did not go now, I might never go. But my mother did not need to know that.

"Sweetheart, I don't want to come in between your dreams."

I brushed the side of my mom's face with my hand, her skin clammy to the touch. "You aren't. I promise."

***

Once my mother was discharged, our life changed drastically. Responsibility was pressed upon my shoulders as I balanced the demands of caring for my mother and the necessity of keeping our household afloat. It had been a few weeks since her diagnosis, and life had become a delicate dance of tending to her needs while juggling the burdens of everyday life.

Cooking, cleaning, and running errands had become my daily routine. But in the face of mounting hospital bills, I knew I needed to do more. That's why I had taken up a job at the local diner, named Grace's Place, to ensure that we could continue to make ends meet.

Amid my hectic schedule, I found myself at the town's pharmacy, standing in line to fill one of my mother's prescriptions. The familiar scent of medicine filled the air, mingling with the sound of customers murmuring their own stories of health and healing.

Finally, it was my turn. I approached the counter, clutching the prescription in my hands. The pharmacist, a kind-eyed man named Mr. Jenkins, greeted me with a warm smile.

"Hello, dear. I see you're here to pick up your mother's medication."

I nodded, offering a small smile in return. "Yes, it's an anti-nausea medication. She's been having a tough time with the side effects of the treatment."

Mr. Jenkins reached for the prescription and began processing it. As he typed away on the computer, I couldn't help but feel a glimmer of hope that this medication would bring some relief to my mother, even if just a little.

After a few moments, Mr. Jenkins turned to me, his expression apologetic. "I'm afraid we're currently running low on stock for that medication. It will only be a little while before we can fill it. Would you mind running a few errands and coming back later?"

A pang of disappointment tugged at my heart, but I understood that sometimes these things were beyond our control. "Of course, Mr. Jenkins. I'll run a few errands and be back as soon as I can."

With a grateful nod, I left the pharmacy, my mind already

shifting gears, mapping out things I could do to pass the time since it made no sense to return home in the meantime.

As I snapped out of my thoughts, my gaze wandered up and landed on a peculiar sight. A bookshop, nestled among the row of buildings, stood before me, its antiquated appearance contrasting with the modern surroundings.

How had I never noticed it before?

Intrigue swelled within me, a magnetic pull drawing me toward the mysterious shop. Curiosity danced in my eyes as I stepped across the threshold, the door's bell tinkling, announcing my arrival. The air inside was heavy with the scent of old books, a fragrance that enveloped me like a comforting embrace.

The bookshelves, reaching towards the ceiling, held volumes upon volumes of literary treasures. Dust particles floated in the warm glow of the dim lighting. I felt a sense of wonder and nostalgia, as though stepping into a different era altogether.

There, amidst the rows of books, a particular shelf caught my attention. It beckoned me closer, whispering secrets only I could hear. Following the invisible thread of curiosity, I traced my fingers along the spines until I found myself inexplicably drawn to a small, green book without a title. Its worn cover held an air of mystery as if it held within its pages something extraordinary.

Without hesitating, I plucked the book from its resting place, cradling it in my hands. As I opened it, a surge of anticipation coursed through my veins. But as soon as the pages touched my fingertips, a strange sensation rippled through me. It was as though the world around me compressed, folding in on itself.

Suddenly, everything went dark. The book slipped from my grasp, disappearing into the void. Panic gripped my heart as I realized I, too, had vanished.

3

A Carriage

As I materialized in the middle of a dusty pathway, the air thick with the scent of horse manure and the distant sound of hooves pounding against the ground, I was overcome with a bewildering sense of displacement. Confusion clouded my thoughts as I attempted to comprehend the impossible. How had I traveled through space?

Before I could process my surroundings, the deafening clatter of a horse-drawn carriage barreled toward me, ripping me from my daze. Instinct took hold as I lunged out of harm's way, the adrenaline coursing through my veins heightening my senses.

My body collided with the ground, a sharp jolt shooting through my skull as my head made contact with the unforgiving earth. Pain radiated through me, causing my vision to blur. Disoriented and disheveled, I found myself lying in a patch of grass, my head spinning with pain and bewilderment.

The carriage came to a sudden halt, the sound of creaking wood and the clatter of hooves filling the air. My heart pounded in my chest as I tried to steady my breath, the realization of the close call sinking in. I was fortunate to have avoided a disastrous collision.

As the commotion settled, the carriage door swung open, and a young man, no older than twenty, emerged from within. His attire was that of a gentleman of the 18th century, a waistcoat and breeches adorning his figure. His eyes widened as they fell upon me.

"What in blazes do you think you're doing, madam?" he exclaimed, his gaze sweeping over me.

Still trying to regain my composure, I managed to utter a shaky response, "I... I'm sorry. I don't know how I ended up here."

His concern softened his features as he observed my disheveled state and the trickle of blood on my forehead. He closed the distance between us, kneeling beside me.

"You're hurt." I detected a hint of worry in his voice; I must have looked a fright. "Let me assist you."

With gentle hands, he reached for a handkerchief tucked within his waistcoat and pressed it against the wound on my forehead. The touch of his hand sent a comforting warmth through me, momentarily easing the pain.

"I must apologize for my brusque manner earlier," he continued, his tone sincere. "I was taken aback by your sudden appearance and the perilous situation."

His concern and kindness touched me, reminding me that despite the temporal divide, compassion was a timeless virtue.

With a grateful smile, I replied, "Thank you for your concern. I didn't mean to cause any trouble."

He offered me a hand, helping me to my feet. His gaze met mine, searching for reassurance. "Do you have a place to stay? I would be remiss to leave you unattended."

I shook my head, realizing that I had been deposited in this unfamiliar time without any belongings or means of sustenance. "No, I don't. I'm afraid I'm at a loss."

His eyes softened. "I cannot leave you stranded. Please, allow me to accompany you to my estate where you can rest and regain your strength. We can discuss your situation further and determine a way to assist you."

As the young man extended the courtesy of introducing himself, revealing his name to be Leo Abernathy, I reciprocated with a polite smile. The situation started to settle upon me as I stood there, an anomaly in this distant era.

Leo Abernathy's eyes drifted to my attire, his brow furrowing in contemplation. "Pray tell, madam, your garments and accent appear foreign to these lands. From where do you hail?"

I took a moment to gather my thoughts, careful not to divulge too much about my true origin. "I am from America." I hoped to offer a vague answer. After all, revealing the truth of time travel seemed implausible and could only complicate matters further.

Recognition flashed across Leo Abernathy's face, his expression reflecting a blend of understanding and surprise. "Ah, from the colonies," he mused, his tone reflecting a touch of admiration. "Quite a journey you must have embarked upon. My travels have not yet taken me to those distant shores."

A wave of relief washed over me, grateful that my response had not raised further suspicion. As Leo Abernathy extended his arm, a gesture of chivalry and assistance, I accepted. With his guidance, I stepped into the waiting carriage, mindful of my injured head. The plush interior enveloped me in comfort, providing respite from the unfamiliar surroundings.

Leo Abernathy's authoritative voice rang out, addressing the driver. "Take us home, James."

"Yes, Sir. But... Sir. I swear, I did not see her. She appeared out of nowhere which is why I had to swerve. Do give my apologies to the lady."

"I shall deliver them." Leo Abernathy nodded to the driver before entering the carriage.

The carriage jolted into motion, its wheels turning against the uneven road, while Leo Abernathy settled into a seat beside me. The rhythmic clatter of hooves against the cobblestones reverberated through the carriage, a lulling cadence that slowly eased my nerves.

As we traveled along, I couldn't help but steal glances at the passing landscapes, the quaint countryside unfolding before my eyes. The timeless beauty of the rolling hills and the architecture of the period painted a picturesque scene, a stark contrast to the world I had left behind.

Silence settled between us, a companionable quiet, broken only by the intermittent clip-clop of the horses' hooves. Lost in my thoughts, I contemplated the implications of this unexpected journey. How would I navigate this foreign time? Would I find a way back to my time? The uncertainties weighed upon me; I could not leave my mother alone.

The carriage rolled to a gentle stop, the horses snorting

softly as we arrived at our destination—Leo Abernathy's estate. As the door swung open, a sense of anticipation mingled with trepidation coursed through me. This encounter would no doubt shape the path ahead.

I took a deep breath, mustering my resolve, and prepared to embark on this unforeseen chapter in my life. With Leo Abernathy's steady presence by my side, I stepped out of the carriage, ready to face whatever lay in store within the confines of his esteemed estate.

As Leo Abernathy led me through the grand entrance of his estate, I couldn't help but marvel at the opulence that surrounded me. The ornate furnishings and intricate details whispered of a world different from my own.

We stepped into a spacious hallway, where an air of quiet elegance permeated the atmosphere. Leo Abernathy's impressive presence commanded respect, and with a few swift words, he summoned a nearby maid.

"Please, fetch a compress, bandages, and a change of clothes for our guest."

The maid nodded in acknowledgment, her eyes glancing in my direction before disappearing to fulfill Leo Abernathy's request. In the meantime, he guided me up a grand staircase, its steps creaking under our weight. Ascending to the first floor, we arrived at a guest room, its door ajar.

With a gentle hand at the small of my back, Leo Abernathy assisted me onto the plush comfort of the bed. Its softness enveloped me, offering a break from the tumultuous events that had transpired. The room exuded a welcoming warmth, allowing me to forget the uncertainties that plagued my mind for a moment.

"I will be just down the hall, Miss Scott." His voice carried a soothing undertone. "Should you need anything, do not hesitate to call upon me."

His strong jawline, defined and chiseled, added a touch of masculinity to his overall allure. It was a jawline that exuded confidence and strength, yet softened by a gentle smile that could melt even the coldest of hearts. It was impossible for me not to be captivated by his presence, by the way he commanded attention in any room he entered.

But it wasn't just his physical appearance that captivated me. It was the way he carried himself, with a mixture of grace and self-assurance. His presence radiated magnetic energy that drew people towards him, and I found myself irresistibly drawn to him.

I offered a grateful smile, appreciative of his attentiveness and hospitality while he waited for the maid to arrive.

Moments later, the door opened once again, and the maid entered, a tray in her hands. She placed it on a nearby table, her gaze lingering on my injured forehead with sympathy and determination.

I nodded to Leo Abernathy. "Thank you," I replied, signaling that he was free to leave.

Leo Abernathy gestured for the maid to attend to me. "Please, take care of Miss Scott's head wound."

The maid's hands moved with practiced precision, tending to my injury. She cleaned the wound with gentle care, applying a cool compress to alleviate the pain. The bandages were expertly wrapped, ensuring the wound was protected and allowed to heal.

"Thank you," I told the maid.

The maid smiled at me as she lifted her fingers from the bandage around my head. "It isn't too tight? You must let me know if it is so I can adjust it."

I shook my head wincing at the movement. "No, it feels secure but not too tight."

"Good. If there is anything else you should require, please do not hesitate to send for me."

As the maid completed her task, she offered me another kind smile before quietly exiting the room, leaving me in the solitude of my thoughts once more.

I reclined on the bed, feeling a comforting coolness against my forehead, the throbbing sensation gradually subsiding. The quiet stillness of the room enveloped me, granting me a moment of reprieve amidst the whirlwind of emotions that accompanied my temporal displacement.

Grateful for Leo Abernathy's hospitality and the care extended to me, I closed my eyes, allowing the weariness to settle in.

As the throbbing in my head persisted, my thoughts drifted to my mother, her illness looming in the forefront of my mind. The weight of responsibility pressed upon me, knowing that her well-being relied on my return. How would she cope if I were unable to make my way back to her? The uncertainty gnawed at my heart, fueling my determination to find a solution.

A tinge of resentment seeped into my thoughts as I pondered the mysterious bookshop, now vanished from sight. Accusing it of witchcraft felt like a desperate attempt to rationalize the inexplicable. The allure and peculiarity of that place lingered, its very existence serving as a tantalizing enigma that demanded further exploration.

But for now, my focus had to shift. I needed to devise a plan to navigate this foreign time, one that would lead me back to the familiar embrace of my time. Determination coursed through my veins as I resolved to seek answers and forge a path forward.

My musings turned to the year in which I now found myself. Abernathy's attire, reminiscent of the 18th century, suggested a timeline steeped in history. Yet, without concrete evidence or knowledge of the current year, my assumptions remained speculative at best. I needed more information to ascertain my whereabouts.

An idea began to take shape in my mind, a plan to gather clues and uncover the truth. Research, observation, and perhaps even discreet conversations with those around me would be necessary to piece together the puzzle of time.

Drawing upon a newfound well of resolve, I pushed aside the fear and uncertainty that threatened to overwhelm me. I would not let myself be confined to the past but rather use it as a stepping stone toward my ultimate goal. My mother's health and my survival depended on it.

Taking a deep breath, I sat up on the bed, my head still tender but my determination unyielding. The room around me, so different from the world I knew, pulsed with history and possibility. It was a reminder that despite the challenges I faced, there was a wealth of untapped knowledge waiting to be discovered.

The throbbing pain in my head persisted, a reminder of the disorienting journey that had brought me to this unfamiliar time. As I shifted my gaze toward the clothing left for me by the maid, draped over the back of a nearby chair, a spark of curiosity ignited within me.

With careful movements, mindful of the ache in my head, I rose from the bed and made my way toward the chair. My fingers grazed the fabric, feeling the texture of another time beneath my touch. The ensemble before me bore the distinct mark of the 18th century, a style elegant but cumbersome.

A wave of uncertainty washed over me. Would changing into these period clothes aid me in my quest for answers? Could it provide me with the means to explore the estate more freely, to gather the knowledge I sought without arousing suspicion?

I shed my contemporary attire, folding it and placing it aside. As I began to slip into the 18th-century garments, I marveled at their intricacy and attention to detail. Each button and delicate stitch transported me further back in time, urging me to embrace the role I now found myself in.

With a final adjustment of the ensemble, I stood before the mirror, my reflection a vision from another era. The gown enveloped me, its soft fabric cascading down to the floor, and I couldn't help but feel a newfound sense of belonging. In this attire, I would be less conspicuous, better able to navigate the estate and seek the answers I sought.

The throbbing in my head forgotten, I took a deep breath and steeled myself for the journey ahead. It was time to venture beyond the confines of my temporary sanctuary, to explore the estate and unravel the mysteries that lay in wait.

As I cast a final glance toward the room that had offered me solace, I left behind the remnants of my former self.

Embracing the unknown, I stepped out into the estate, ready to discover the truths that awaited me in this unfamiliar era.

4

A Piano Forte

With each step I took, I strained my ears, listening for any signs of movement or voices in the hallway. Leo. Abernathy's words echoed in my mind, reminding me of the proximity of his room. I couldn't afford to be discovered; my exploration had to remain discreet.

Tiptoeing through the dimly lit corridor, I made an effort to keep my movements as silent as possible. The ancient floorboards creaked beneath my weight, my heart pounding in my chest as I navigated the unfamiliar territory. Every instinct screamed at me to proceed with caution, to ensure that my presence went unnoticed.

As my eyes scanned the hallway, I noticed a door ajar. Curiosity coursed through me, drawing me towards its mysterious allure. What secrets might lie beyond that narrow opening? It was a risk I was willing to take in my quest for answers.

Approaching the doorway with measured steps, I peered

inside, revealing a study adorned with shelves lined with weathered books and antique trinkets.

Taking a tentative step forward, I entered the study, my eyes scanning the room for any indication of the date. Dust particles danced in the sunlight that streamed through the window, creating an ethereal atmosphere. The musty scent of old parchment mingled with the lingering scent of polished wood, evoking a sense of nostalgia.

I moved closer to a sturdy wooden desk, examining the papers and objects scattered across its surface. My fingers grazed the worn edges of an open book, its yellowed pages revealing passages of wisdom from centuries past. Though the words held their own allure, I couldn't find the concrete information I sought within its aged confines.

My gaze shifted, landing on a carved wooden calendar hanging on the study wall. I approached it cautiously, my eyes scouring the marked dates. My heart skipped a beat as I focused on the numbers and symbols etched into its surface.

My eyes widened as I traced my finger over the calendar's surface. The dates matched the 18th-century timeline that I had suspected, confirming my initial observations. Though it provided no exact date, I returned my attention to the desk where more papers waited to be searched.

My mouth dropped open as I scanned the dates on the stack of ledgers, seeking a clue that would anchor me to the present moment. And there it was, written in faded ink: July 14th, 1764. A surge of relief and uncertainty washed over me. I had found a date, but what significance did it hold? The page held a note about raising taxes, but the context was unclear.

Lost in my thoughts, I was startled when a deep, male voice resonated from behind me.

"And who might this be?"

My heart skipped a beat as I turned, finding myself face-to-face with a middle-aged man, clothed and coiffed impeccably. Panic clenched at my chest as I tried to gather my wits, searching for a plausible explanation for my presence in this study.

I forced myself to respond calmly. "I... I was looking for Leo Abernathy. I needed to speak with him." The words slipped from my lips, my mind racing to maintain composure and avoid arousing further suspicion.

The man regarded me with a scrutinizing gaze, his brows furrowing. "Why would you need to find my son?" Now that he mentioned it, I could see the resemblance. Leo Abernathy resembled his father, with the same jawline and full head of hair. The only difference was a couple of decades in age.

Before I could conjure a response, Leo Abernathy materialized at his father's side. "Father, I heard voices and came to investigate." He glanced at me, his eyes flitting over the bandage on my head wound before returning his gaze to his father. "I apologize for the intrusion. It was my fault that Rosemary injured her head, and I brought her here to ensure she received proper care. I told her to come look for me if she needed anything; she must have gotten lost."

"That is right." A wave of relief washed over me as I seized the opportunity, realizing that his quick thinking could shield me from further scrutiny.

Leo Abernathy's father studied us both for a moment, his expression softening with understanding. "Very well. Ensure

Rosemary receives the attention she needs, and see that she is comfortable during her stay."

I nodded, my heart still racing with the close call. "Thank you, sir." My voice sounded thin, as if a gust of wind could blow it away. It was a delicate dance of secrets and trust, and I couldn't afford to stumble.

With a nod of acknowledgment, Leo Abernathy's father turned and exited the study, leaving Leo Abernathy and me alone. I exhaled, my shoulders sagging with relief.

Leo Abernathy approached me, concern etched across his features. "Are you all right? Was there anything you needed?"

I offered a genuine smile to Leo Abernathy. "It wasn't anything important; I wanted to thank you for your assistance and for taking care of me. I appreciate your quick thinking and for getting your maid to look after me."

Leo Abernathy returned my smile, his eyes sparkling with warmth. "It was my pleasure, Miss Rosemary. How does your head feel?"

"It still throbs a bit, but the compress is helping."

"I'm relieved that you're starting to feel better."

As we stood there in the first-floor hallway, Leo Abernathy's next words caught me by surprise. "If you're feeling well enough, would you care to join me for a bite to eat? I, for one, haven't had tea, and I can only assume that you would like some food as well."

I hesitated for a moment, considering his offer. The allure of exploring this unfamiliar time alongside Leo Abernathy intrigued me, and his company provided a sense of comfort. "I'd be glad to join you." I felt a smile tugging at the corners of my lips.

Together, we made our way down the grand staircase, Leo Abernathy's presence beside me grounding me amidst the grandeur of his ancestral home. He called out to a passing maid, instructing her to bring refreshments to the parlor.

As we entered the parlor, my eyes were drawn to the exquisite pianoforte nestled in the corner. Its polished wood and intricate details beckoned to me, filling my heart with longing.

Leo Abernathy noticed my gaze. "Do you play?"

A rush of excitement coursed through me, and I nodded. "Yes, I do. It's one of my greatest passions."

A smile curved on Leo Abernathy's lips. "I hope I'll get the chance to hear you play someday."

"Perhaps." The possibilities swirled through my head. If I thought about what could happen in the future, it meant that I had not found a way back to my own time.

Leo Abernathy guided me to a small couch, and he settled into a chair across from me. Our conversation flowed easily as we waited for a maid to bring the food.

The same maid who had attended to my bandaged forehead entered the parlor, carrying a tray. She approached me with a warm smile.

"How does your bandage feel, Miss Rosemary?"

I touched the bandage, reassuring her with a nod. "It feels fine, thank you."

The maid set down the tray and arranged the refreshments, then left us alone. I was surprised at how easy Leo Abernathy was to talk to. I did not know that much about 18th-century England but had imagined stiff men who barely acknowledged women.

How wrong I was.

Leo Abernathy opened up, his eyes sparkling as he recounted a tale from his childhood.

"It was during the summers on our estate," he began, a hint of mischief in his smile. "My dear friend, Jonathan—the butler's son—and I would find ourselves in the most delightful adventures. We were like peas in a pod, always getting into some sort of mischief."

I leaned forward, completely engrossed in his storytelling, eager to hear more about the escapades of Leo Abernathy's youth. The parlor came alive with his animated gestures and vivid descriptions.

"We used to explore every nook and cranny of the estate. From secret passages hidden behind bookshelves to hidden treasures buried in the gardens, there was never a dull moment. We were relentless in our quest for adventure."

I chuckled, captivated by his enthusiasm. It was as if I could envision the mischievous young boys, sneaking around the estate with wide-eyed curiosity.

"One time," he continued, a mischievous glint in his eyes, "Jonathan and I decided to venture into the forbidden attic. Rumor had it that it was haunted, but that only added to our determination. Armed with candles and a sense of daring, we climbed the creaky staircase, determined to uncover its secrets."

Leo Abernathy's words painted a vivid picture in my mind, and I found myself smiling, eager to hear the outcome of their escapade.

"As it turned out, the attic held no ghostly apparitions, but it did house a collection of old trinkets and dusty furniture.

We spent hours playing make-believe, turning that attic into a pirate's hideout, or a grand castle filled with knights and princesses."

His story transported me to a different time, a time of youthful imagination and carefree adventures. It was a welcome distraction from my predicament.

"I'll always cherish those memories." A wistful smile graced his lips. "Jonathan and I remained friends, even as we grew older. Though now I do not get to see him very often when my father wants me to take a larger role in running the estate. Father has been trying to get me to join him on the board of trade and plantations." Mr. Abernathy chuckled and sipped some of his tea. "Never mind my musings, I doubt you are interested in my working prospects. Please tell me about yourself. How did you end up on our driveway after traveling from the colonies?"

As I contemplated how to approach the subject of my sudden appearance in Leo Abernathy's driveway, a delightful distraction arrived in the form of a young girl and her governess. The girl's eyes sparkled with excitement as she bounded towards Leo Abernathy, her brother, exclaiming his name with pure joy.

"Leo! Leo!" Her voice was filled with infectious enthusiasm. "Look who's here. A new guest."

I watched as Leo Abernathy's face lit up with a warm smile, his attention instantly captured by his younger sister. My worries took a backseat as I observed their interaction, intrigued by the bond between siblings.

"Ah, Amelia," Leo Abernathy greeted her, bending down

to her level. "This is Rosemary. She's a guest at our estate. Rosemary, meet my spirited little sister, Amelia."

I offered Amelia a friendly smile, appreciating her genuine excitement. "It's a pleasure to meet you, Amelia. Mr. Abernathy has been most kind to me."

Leo Abernathy smiled at me. "You can call me Leo."

I nodded, returning his smile and testing his name. "All right...Leo."

Amelia's eyes widened as she regarded me, her mind seemingly brimming with questions. It was as if a world of possibilities had opened up before her in the form of a new friend.

"Rosemary, how did you get here?" Amelia waited on my answer, the governess standing by her side.

I exchanged a glance with Leo Abernathy, knowing I couldn't reveal the truth about my inexplicable arrival in their time, for fear of being misunderstood or causing undue alarm.

"Well, Amelia..." I tried choosing my words carefully. "I was exploring the surroundings, and I happened to take a wrong turn. Luckily, your brother found me and brought me to safety."

Amelia's eyes widened, satisfied with my explanation.

"You're very lucky, Rosemary. We have the best adventures here. I'm certain I can show you all the secret spots, or I can show you what I can do on the pianoforte. My music teacher left a few weeks ago, but I still remember what we were practicing. Father says he will find me a new teacher soon. Would you like me to show you?"

5

A New Student

As Amelia's fingers danced across the piano keys, I couldn't help but admire her determination and enthusiasm. Her youthful exuberance was infectious, and I found myself captivated by her genuine love for music. However, Leo Abernathy's concern for my well-being prompted him to intervene.

"Amelia, perhaps we should let Rosemary rest a bit. She hurt her head earlier, remember?"

Amelia paused, her fingers hovering above the keys, and turned towards me with a hopeful expression. Her genuine desire to share her talent with me tugged at my heart.

"Rosemary, can't you just listen? I promise I won't play too loudly." Amelia's gaze brimmed with anticipation.

I considered Leo Abernathy's concern and weighed it against Amelia's innocent request. I decided that indulging her passion would be a small price to pay for the joy it would bring her.

Smiling, I reassured them both, "It's all right. Really. I'm feeling better now, and I would love to hear you play, Amelia."

Amelia's face lit up with a radiant smile, her eagerness uncontainable. She wasted no time in resuming her position at the pianoforte, her small hands landing somewhat heavily on the keys. The resulting melody was charmingly imperfect, a testament to her youthful enthusiasm and still-developing skills.

As Amelia played, Leo Abernathy leaned closer to me, his voice lowered so only I could hear. Curiosity gleamed in his eyes as he asked about my circumstances.

"Rosemary, forgive my curiosity, but I couldn't help but wonder—do you have a place to stay or family nearby? Should I send word to someone for you?"

I contemplated his questions for a moment, realizing that I needed to fabricate a plausible story to maintain the guise of my purpose in this unfamiliar time. With a composed expression, I replied, "I'm afraid I don't have any lodgings yet, and my family is quite distant. That's actually why I came here—to look for work."

Leo Abernathy nodded understandingly, his features reflecting both sympathy and a desire to assist. We lapsed into a comfortable silence, fully engrossed in Amelia's recital.

As Amelia's music filled the air, I allowed myself to be swept away by the innocence and joy that radiated from her. The imperfections in her performance only added to its charm, and I found myself smiling at the pure delight she took in sharing her talent.

As Amelia's final notes faded into the air, she turned to me with sparkling eyes, her excitement palpable. "Do you play, Rosemary? Can we hear you play the piano too?"

I couldn't help but smile at her eager request, touched by her genuine interest. The camaraderie that had begun to form between us encouraged me to share my musical talents. With a nod, I agreed, "Of course, Amelia. I'd be happy to play for you."

Leo Abernathy, quick with a quip, chimed in, "Well, it seems the chance to hear you play has come sooner than expected, Rosemary."

I chuckled, feeling a warmth blossom within me at his lighthearted comment. Our shared laughter, the way his eyes crinkled at the corners, sparked a connection that I hadn't anticipated. It was as if, at that moment, we understood each other on a deeper level.

With Amelia's encouragement, I made my way to the piano, my heart pounding and palms turning slick. I couldn't deny the growing attraction I felt towards Mr. Abernathy, and being able to showcase my skills on the piano was an opportunity to share a part of myself with him.

Glancing through a leaflet of scores, I selected a piece that was both beautiful and challenging. It required precision and dexterity, but it also carried an emotional depth that resonated with me. As I positioned my fingers on the keys, I took a deep breath and began to play.

The room fell into a hushed silence as the melodies flowed from my fingertips. Years of practice and love for the piano guided me, allowing me to express my emotions through each carefully crafted note. The music filled the space, captivating the hearts and minds of those around me.

As I played, I stole glances at Leo Abernathy, his gaze fixed on me with awe and admiration. Our eyes met, and in that shared connection, I could sense a mutual appreciation and attraction. It was as if the music had brought us closer, bridging the gap between our worlds and allowing us to understand each other in a way that words couldn't convey.

The last lingering note hung in the air, and the room erupted in applause. I smiled, feeling a sense of accomplishment and gratification. The warmth in Leo Abernathy's eyes only deepened, and I found myself longing to know more about him, to explore the depths of our connection further.

As the final echoes of the applause faded away, I couldn't help but feel a sense of contentment wash over me. The room was still filled with the lingering emotions of the music, and Leo Abernathy's words of admiration only added to the warmth that filled my heart.

"Rosemary, I must admit, I hadn't anticipated such magnificent playing from you." His masculine voice was laced with genuine awe. "Your talents go far beyond what most gentlewomen possess."

I blushed at his praise, my cheeks tinged with a rosy hue. "Thank you, Mr. Aber—I mean, Leo." It was strange how quickly our familiarity had grown, how easily I had adjusted to using his given name.

Leo's eyes sparkled. "Rosemary, please, remember to call me Leo. There's no need for formality between us."

I nodded, a small smile playing at the corners of my lips. His insistence on using his first name only served to strengthen the connection that had been forming between us. It felt as though we were sharing a secret, an unspoken understanding that something was blossoming between us in this unexpected encounter.

My worries and the uncertainty of my circumstances faded into the background. The comfort and familiarity I found in Leo's presence allowed me to forget the time traveler's predicament I had found myself in.

As we exchanged glances, unspoken words danced between us. There was a magnetic pull, an undeniable attraction that neither of us could ignore. In Leo's eyes, I saw a reflection of my curiosity and longing. It was as if we both yearned to explore this newfound connection and see where it would lead us.

I realized that our meeting was not merely a chance encounter but a turning point in both our lives. The melodies I had played on the piano had not only captivated those who listened but had woven a delicate thread between Leo and me, binding us together in a shared journey.

With a gentle nod and a whispered promise to remember his request, I allowed myself to bask in the warmth of Leo's gaze.

Amelia's youthful enthusiasm broke the enchanting spell that had enveloped Leo and me, reminding us of the world beyond our shared connection. She bounced up and down, her eyes shining with excitement as she turned to Leo.

"Leo, can Rosemary be my new piano teacher?"

I glanced at Leo, unsure of how to respond. Teaching had never been a part of my plans or aspirations. I had always considered myself a student of music, not a teacher. But as I met Leo's gaze, curiosity and consideration ignited within me.

"I... I'm not a teacher, Amelia. I've never taught piano before."

Leo's thoughtful expression filled the room, his eyes searching mine. "Rosemary, you said you were looking for work. Why not consider working as a piano teacher?"

His words took me by surprise, and I found myself caught in a whirlwind of thoughts and possibilities. Teaching piano could provide me with stability and a purpose during my unexpected stay in this unfamiliar time. It could also allow me to remain close to Leo, unraveling the layers of our connection with each lesson.

Moreover, Leo's suggestion meant that I wouldn't have to search for separate lodgings, maintaining the convenience of staying within the estate. The thought of continuing to occupy the guest room provided a sense of comfort amidst the uncertainties that lay ahead.

Leo's concern for my well-being, reflected in his desire to ensure the maid's continued care, touched my heart. It was evident that he carried a genuine sense of responsibility for my safety and recovery.

After a moment of contemplation, I met Leo's gaze with a soft smile. "You make a compelling case, Leo. Though I have never considered teaching before, perhaps it is an opportunity worth exploring."

Amelia clapped her hands together, her eyes gleaming with delight. "Oh, I can't wait to start my lessons with you, Rosemary!"

I chuckled, grateful for Amelia's infectious enthusiasm.

"We'll have to see how it goes, Amelia. But I promise to do my best."

We remained in the parlor for a while, sipping a now lukewarm tea and polishing off the remaining bits of food, before Leo suggested I should retire to my room and get some rest. He must have noticed that I kept clutching the side of my head as the throbbing in my skull heightened.

As I entered the tranquility of my guest room, the events of the day still swirled in my mind. The maid had kindly left a bowl of water for me, and I appreciated her assistance in helping me navigate the intricacies of 18th-century clothing. Her comment on the poorly fastened garments made me chuckle to myself, realizing just how out of place I must appear.

Once the maid bid me goodnight and left the room, I found solace in the simple act of undressing, exchanging the restrictive layers for a comfortable shift. I gazed at my reflection in the mirror of the armoire, my brown curly hair cascading around my shoulders. The water in the bowl beckoned to me, and I dipped my fingers into it, splashing the cool liquid on my face to freshen up.

As I patted my face dry with a nearby towel, my thoughts turned to my mother, who had to be worried about my absence. Her illness had burdened our lives, and now I had added another layer of concern by disappearing without a trace. I yearned to be by her side, offering comfort and support.

My mind then drifted to my brother, serving his duty in Vietnam. I wondered how he was faring, if he was safe and healthy amidst the turmoil of war. Their absence bore heavily on my heart, a reminder of the responsibilities and ties that tethered me to my own time.

But the pressing questions remained: How did I end up here? What mysterious force had transported me through time? And most importantly, how could I find a way back?

A sense of frustration gnawed at me as I surveyed the room, searching for any clue or connection to the peculiar bookshop. Yet, everything within this elegant estate bore no resemblance to the enigmatic shop I had entered earlier. It seemed as if that door had closed behind me, leaving me with no tangible leads to pursue.

With a sigh, I finished braiding my hair and set the bowl of water aside. As I settled into the embrace of the soft bed, I stared up at the ceiling, the flickering candlelight casting dancing shadows across the room. Uncertainty loomed over me, but I vowed to remain resilient and to continue seeking answers and solutions in this unfamiliar era.

Tomorrow would bring new opportunities and challenges. The maid's promise of assistance and the prospect of teaching piano to Amelia filled me with hope. Perhaps within these connections and responsibilities lay the path back to my own time.

With that thought lingering in my mind, I closed my eyes, offering a silent prayer for guidance and protection for my loved ones.

6

⧼◈⧽

Fresh Air

Amelia, brimming with enthusiasm, perched on the piano bench beside me, her eyes sparkling with anticipation. I couldn't help but smile at her eagerness to learn. Her governess, a petite redhead with a kind and observant gaze, sat in a nearby chair, stitching her clothing. The gentle sound of needle and thread added a soothing rhythm to the room.

"Shall we begin, Amelia?" My fingers poised over the keys. She nodded, her curls bouncing with each movement. I started with the foundations, teaching her the importance of hand positioning and the placement of fingers on the keys. We practiced scales and basic exercises, building a solid musical foundation.

Amelia's determination and natural talent shone through as she absorbed each lesson. Her fingers danced across the keys, a testament to her growing skill. It was a joy to witness her progress and witness the spark of music ignite within her.

The governess, her nimble fingers navigating the needle, occasionally glanced up from her work to observe our interaction.

As the morning unfolded, the parlor filled with the harmonious sounds of music mingled with the soft rustling of fabric. The basket at the governess's feet brimmed with an assortment of colorful fabrics and spools of thread, a testament to her resourcefulness and industriousness.

Between lessons and demonstrations, I found moments to exchange friendly conversations with the governess.

As the lessons drew to a close, Amelia beamed with satisfaction, eager to practice on her own. I praised her efforts while the governess returned the fabric and thread to the basket near her feet.

"Come on, Amelia. It is time for your next class." The governess stood, lifting the basket with one arm.

Amelia pouted. "Already? But we just got started. Can we skip math today?"

The governess shook her head though she wasn't able to hide a smile creeping up her face." Let us go to your classroom. You do not want me to tell your father that you have been ignoring your studies, right?"

"Alright, Miss Lucy." Amelia sounded disappointed but she got up nonetheless and followed the governess out of the parlor.

With Amelia and the governess having left the parlor, a sense of tranquility settled upon the room. I touched the bandage on my forehead, feeling the slight tenderness beneath my fingertips. The small cut had scabbed over, evidence of the accident that had brought me to this place. I could probably take the bandage off tomorrow.

Lost in thought, I pondered my next course of action. I could use some fresh air to clear my mind and a chance to explore the surroundings, hoping to uncover any clues, however slim, that might lead me back to my own time.

Stepping away from the piano, I made my way toward the grand entrance of the estate. The wooden doors creaked as I pushed them open, revealing a world of greenery and sunlight beyond.

A gentle breeze caressed my face as I stepped outside, carrying with it the scents of blooming flowers and the earthy fragrance of the countryside. The vast expanse of the estate stretched before me.

The beauty of the estate's grounds captivated me—a picturesque landscape adorned with vibrant flowers, towering trees, and meandering paths that enticed exploration.

I strolled along the winding pathways, my footsteps cushioned by the soft earth beneath. Birds serenaded me with their melodic songs, and the distant sound of a babbling brook added a soothing symphony to the scene. It was a welcome respite from my own time though I felt guilty to admit it.

As I meandered further, my curiosity led me to a small rose garden. The delicate petals in various shades of red and pink bloomed with life, their fragrance filling the air. I paused, tracing my fingers along the velvety petals, reveling in their softness.

I continued my exploration, discovering a path that wound its way through a dense thicket. Intrigued, I followed it with a sense of wonder. The dappled sunlight filtered through the foliage, casting enchanting patterns on the forest floor.

I rounded a bend in the path, only to be startled by the sight of a magnificent horse standing before me. It was Leo, mounted on his steed, and my heart skipped a beat at the unexpected encounter. He reined in the horse and dismounted, his concern etched upon his features.

"Rosemary, I nearly caused harm to you once more. What are you doing wandering in the woods?"

His genuine concern touched me, and I offered him a reassuring smile. "I've just finished my lesson with Amelia, and I desired some fresh air."

Leo's gaze softened as he understood my need for solitude. "I enjoy riding across the estate, exploring these very woods." His eyes drifted towards the majestic trees. "If you'd like, we can continue our walk together. It's always better to have company amidst nature's embrace."

I nodded in agreement. Leo tied the horse's reins to a nearby tree, ensuring its safety, and then joined me on the path. Side by side, we continued our meandering journey through the woods.

As we walked, Leo's presence became a source of comfort and companionship. We exchanged anecdotes and observations, our voices blending harmoniously with the rustling leaves, creating an atmosphere of enchantment.

With each step, I found myself opening up to Leo, sharing fragments of my thoughts and aspirations. There was a sense of ease between us as if we were kindred spirits destined to cross paths.

Time became irrelevant.

The beauty of the woods unfolded around us, and we found ourselves at a picturesque spot by a babbling brook. The sound of water cascading over rocks filled the air, a soothing melody that mingled with the rustling leaves.

As Leo and I stood side by side, a palpable tension enveloped us. The air seemed charged with an unspoken longing, and I couldn't help but feel his gaze upon me. I turned to meet his eyes, my heart fluttering within my chest.

His eyes, deep and expressive, held a mix of desire and hesitation. Time stood still as his gaze traversed the distance between us. It lingered on my lips, a fleeting touch that sent shivers down my spine, before returning to meet my gaze once again.

The silence between us was pregnant with unspoken words, the anticipation hanging heavy in the air. I could see the conflict within him, his desire warring with his restraint. A part of me longed for him to close the distance, to bridge the gap that separated us, while another part was filled with uncertainty and apprehension.

My lips tingled, as if echoing his unvoiced desire. I found myself moistening them, mirroring his actions. It was as though an invisible thread connected us, drawing us closer, yet the unknown held us in a delicate balance.

I yearned to know what lay beyond the edge of that precipice. Did he feel the same pull, the same magnetic attraction that stirred within me? Or was it a figment of my imagination, a projection of my desires onto his hesitant gaze?

A breeze rustled through the trees, scattering leaves in its wake as if nature herself was urging us to take that leap, to embrace the unknown. But before either of us could find the courage to act, the spell was broken.

A distant sound reached our ears, the faint call of someone in need of assistance, and the moment dissolved into the fabric of time. We turned our heads, our gazes breaking away from the magnetic pull that had held us captive. It was as if the world had conspired to prevent our lips from meeting, to keep the unspoken words locked within our hearts.

Leo's expression shifted, a mixture of regret and determination crossing his features. With a soft sigh, he tore his gaze away from mine, and we stepped back from the precipice that threatened to consume us.

"We should go."

Did I imagine the hint of disappointment in his voice?

I nodded, my own heart heavy with unspoken desires. We turned away from the brook, leaving the moment behind as we made our way back towards the main building.

As we reached Leo's horse, he suggested that his trusty companion could carry us both back to the estate. With a graceful motion, Leo mounted the horse, his ease and familiarity with the creature evident. He extended a hand towards me, an invitation to join him.

Feeling a mix of excitement and uncertainty, I took his hand and allowed him to pull me up in front of him. My heart quickened as my back pressed against his chest, and a pleasant warmth enveloped me. The closeness was intoxicating, his strong arms holding me securely.

With a gentle nudge, the horse set off, its powerful muscles propelling us forward. We wound our way through the path we had previously traversed, the wind rushing past us. It was a moment of freedom, of letting go, as if the world around us blurred into a hazy backdrop.

As we rode, I couldn't help but steal glances at Leo, his presence behind me comforting and exhilarating at the same time. His steady breath against the nape of my neck sent shivers down my spine, and I found myself leaning back, seeking that connection.

The journey seemed both fleeting and endless, a stolen interlude in time. And as we arrived at the stables, Leo dismounted first, his movements fluid and graceful. With a gentle smile, he reached up, offering his hand to me once again.

Accepting his gesture, I allowed him to lift me down from the horse. The moment our hands touched, a jolt of electricity surged through me, igniting a fire within. I landed on the stable ground, yet my senses were still attuned to the memory of his touch, lingering on my skin.

Leo's eyes met mine, an unspoken understanding passing between us. The world around us faded into the background, leaving only the two of us standing in that moment. It was a moment filled with anticipation as if the air crackled with unspoken desires.

But before anything more could transpire, reality encroached upon us once again. The bustling sounds of the stable workers and the hum of activity brought us back to the present. With a subtle sigh, Leo relinquished his hold on me, though reluctance lingered in his gaze.

"Thank you." My voice was barely audible over the surrounding commotion.

Leo nodded, his eyes reflecting a mixture of emotions. "You're welcome."

With a lingering glance, we silently acknowledged the intensity of our shared experience. Then, we parted ways, each returning to our separate responsibilities within the estate.

As I walked away from the stables, the echoes of our shared ride still reverberating within me, a sense of determination washed over me. I needed to remain focused on my goal—finding a way back to my own time, to my family. I couldn't let the allure of someone like Leo, with his captivating presence and kind demeanor, divert my attention from what needed to be done.

I reminded myself that as much as I enjoyed his company, as drawn as I felt toward him, my purpose here was not to become entangled in a romantic liaison. My heart fluttered at the mere thought of what could be between us, but I had to be cautious. I couldn't allow myself to be swayed by the enchantment of the moment.

With each step I took, I repeated the mantra in my mind. I needed to remain focused, to gather any clues or knowledge that might lead me back to my own time.

I couldn't afford to lose sight of that.

The memory of my family, alone and waiting for my return, tugged at my heartstrings. The weight of responsibility settled upon my shoulders, urging me to press forward. I owed it to them, and to myself, to unravel the enigma that had transported me here and find my way back.

Though my thoughts drifted to Leo, his image seared into my mind, and I reminded myself that this was not the time for distractions. I needed to keep my emotions in check and my focus sharp.

My determination grew stronger. I would explore every

avenue, follow every lead, and unravel the mysteries that lay before me. My journey was far from over, and I couldn't afford to let anything—no matter how enticing—derail me from my mission.

With each stride, I etched this resolve into my very being, vowing to stay true to my purpose. The road ahead might be uncertain, but I was determined to find my way back home, to my family. And nothing, not even the magnetic pull of Leo, could shake that resolve.

7

The Board Of Trade

After closing the lid to cover the keys, I stretched my hands and patted Amelia on her shoulder, congratulating her for another successful piano lesson. Teaching had been a strange but rewarding situation. Mrs. Johnson had made it appear much easier than it was. As we exited the parlor, the echoes of Amelia's piano practice still resonated in the air. The governess, who had introduced herself as Georgiana, Amelia, and I walked side by side, engaging in casual conversation about the progress she had made during her lesson. The sense of accomplishment lingered, filling the air with a touch of satisfaction.

As we prepared to leave the parlor, the atmosphere shifted as the heavy footsteps of men echoed through the hallway. I turned my head to see the senior Mr. Abernathy, Leo's father, leading a group of six distinguished-looking gentlemen. Their conversation carried a weight of importance, snippets of which reached my ears—discussions about trade with the colonies and raised taxes.

What was even going on in 1764? My mind raced back to my high school history classes. I had never really been that interested in history, but I could vaguely remember something about the French-Indian War—didn't that end in 1763? The Revolutionary War wasn't until some eleven years after this time.

Mr. Abernathy, upon noticing our presence, gestured for the men to make themselves comfortable in the parlor. But before joining them, he turned his attention to his son, Leo, who had just arrived. "Leo, why don't you join us in the parlor?"

"Thank you, Father, but I have other matters to attend to at the moment."

The momentary pause that followed was filled with unspoken tension. It seemed that Leo's decision didn't align with his father's expectations, which were veiled within the folds of Mr. Abernathy's disappointed expression.

Undeterred, Mr. Abernathy redirected his attention to an upcoming social event—a dance at Granhope Manor. Excitement tinged his voice as he mentioned the presence of the Earl of Hillsborough, a figure who I assumed was of high importance in the social hierarchy.

"Leo, I do expect you to attend the dance. It's an excellent opportunity to mingle with influential figures, and I wish to introduce you to the earl personally." There was a hint of admonishment in Mr. Abernathy's voice and posture, his expression stern as he gazed at his son.

Leo nodded, his eyes meeting his father's with understanding and reluctance. "I understand, Father. I will make sure to mark it in my calendar."

As an observer of this familial exchange, I couldn't help but be intrigued. The dynamics between Mr. Abernathy and Leo were interesting, and I wondered how their relationship would unfold in the days to come. And as for the upcoming dance, it appeared that the social circle of this time held its own set of expectations and obligations.

Noticing my continued presence, Mr. Abernathy nodded to me. "Miss Scott, a pleasure to see you again. I hear my son has hired you as Amelia's new piano teacher?"

I brightened my smile. "Yes, sir. It is my pleasure. Amelia is a delight to teach."

"Wonderful, wonderful." Mr. Abernathy glanced back, checking on his guests. "I hope you are comfortable. How does your head feel?"

"Much better, sir. I've been able to take the bandage off, and aside from some light bruising which can be hidden by my hair until they're healed"—I pointed to the whorls of brown curls covering my forehead—"I have no lasting issues."

"I'm pleased to hear that. Well... in that case, I shall leave you in the care of my son. I must return to my guests. I'm certain we shall get to speak more at a different time."

With a last nod, Mr. Abernathy entered the parlor and shut the door behind him, leaving Leo and me alone in the hallway.

As we walked away from the parlor, curiosity tugged at my thoughts, and I turned to Leo with genuine inquisitiveness.

"Leo, could you enlighten me about the discussion your

father and the gentlemen were having? It seemed quite important."

Leo glanced at me, his expression thoughtful. "My father serves on the Board of Plantation and Trade," he began, his voice tinged with resignation. "He has always hoped I would follow in his footsteps, but politics have never held much interest for me."

I listened intently, my curiosity piqued. "And who is the Earl of Hillsborough? Your father mentioned him earlier."

Leo nodded, his gaze focused on a distant point. "Wills Hill, the Earl of Hillsborough, is the current President of the Board of Plantation and Trade. His influence in the political sphere is significant, and his decisions hold great weight in matters of commerce."

I couldn't help but sympathize with Leo's predicament. The weight of expectations, the struggle between personal desires and familial obligations—it was a delicate balance that many faced. His gaze met mine, and I could sense a genuine yearning for understanding.

"I find myself torn, Rosemary," Leo confessed, his voice laced with sincerity. "While I have no interest in politics, I could not decline my father's request to attend the dance at Granhope Manor. It's a social event where influential figures gather, and my presence is expected."

His words lingered in the air, and a spark ignited between us, the unspoken connection growing stronger. Leo's eyes held a glimmer of sincerity, a vulnerability that touched my heart.

"And Rosemary," he paused, a hint of anticipation in his voice, "I was wondering if you would accompany me to the dance. It would be much more enjoyable with you by my side."

His invitation took me by surprise, and for a moment, uncertainty swirled within me. "I'm afraid I don't know the dances, and I don't possess the appropriate attire for such an occasion."

Leo's smile was warm and reassuring. "You needn't worry about the dances; I will guide you through them. Or... if I might be so bold, I would like to suggest practicing together in advance. And as for your attire, I assure you, Rosemary, you will be perfect just as you are. Your presence alone will brighten the room."

His words melted the lingering doubts, replacing them with a sense of excitement tinged with vulnerability. Perhaps this dance could be an opportunity, a chance to navigate the intricacies of this time and embrace the unexpected. It was not as if I had a way back to my own time, yet.

Leo seemed to think for a moment. "Although, I can have a maid air out one of my mother's gowns. Even if it is a bit outdated, it should still suit you well."

Now that Leo mentioned his mother, I had seen no evidence of a female presence at his estate. "I could not possibly accept a gown without thanking your mother."

A dark cloud passed across Leo's features, and his gaze turned distant. "I'm afraid that will not be possible. You see, my mother passed away four years ago."

"Oh, I am so sorry." I reached for his hand, squeezing his palm to offer a sense of comfort. "Are you certain I can borrow one of her dresses?"

Leo sighed, straightening his posture as he pulled himself

back together, a smile returning to his face. "Yes, she would have loved to know that her belongings still got used. There are more than enough dresses and other garments left to clothe an entire girls' school.

I chuckled, letting go of Leo's hand. "Then I'll gladly accept."

As we were chatting, we reached the foyer, stopping at the base of the staircase where we could go our separate ways; me to my guest room and Leo on to whatever task he might have planned. But Leo hesitated, his gaze moving between the front door and me.

"Do you have other plans at this moment?" He waited on my answer with a curious expression, our meeting gaze sending a tingling down my spine.

"No." I shook my head while keeping his gaze.

"Will you practice dancing with me?" He flashed me a smile that sent a startling sensation through my chest.

Leo's invitation to practice the dances filled me with excitement and nervousness. As we made our way through the estate, my eyes widened in awe at the opulence that surrounded us. Leo led me to a separate wing, and as we entered the grand ballroom, I couldn't help but marvel at its magnificence. The room seemed to come alive with its polished floors, grand chandeliers, and expansive space waiting to be filled with music and laughter.

In the center of the room, Leo turned to face me, his eyes gleaming with anticipation. With a graceful bow, he extended his hand towards me, a silent invitation for a dance. I hesitated for a moment, feeling a flutter of excitement mingled with uncertainty.

"But Leo, there's no music." Amusement laced my voice.

A mischievous smile danced upon his lips. "I can make the music happen."

And with that, he began to hum a light, lively tune, his voice filling the room with a melody that materialized out of thin air. The simplicity of the moment and Leo's playfulness brought forth a giggle from deep within me.

Accepting his hand, I allowed myself to be drawn closer to him. As our bodies moved in sync, guided by an invisible rhythm, I marveled at the ease with which Leo led, his steps sure and confident. He kept perfect pace with the tune he hummed.

The dance steps were intricate, and despite my best efforts, I made a few missteps along the way. But Leo was there, his touch gentle yet firm as he guided me through the intricate patterns.

With each correction, his touch sent shivers down my spine. I found myself drawn to his warm gaze and the way his lips curved into a reassuring smile. There was an undeniable chemistry between us, a magnetic pull that intensified with each passing moment.

Leo's patience and grace made me feel at ease, allowing me to relax into the dance. His strong presence enveloped me, and I found myself moving in sync with him. It was as if our bodies were attuned to one another, responding to the subtle cues and rhythm of the music.

As the music swelled and the dance reached its crescendo, our bodies were close together, almost touching. I could feel the heat radiating from Leo, his masculine scent mingling with the fragrance of the room. The tension between us was palpable, electrifying the air around us.

For a fleeting moment, it seemed as though Leo leaned in, his gaze filled with desire. My heart raced, anticipation building as I wondered if he would finally bridge the gap between us. His hand pressed against the small of my back, its presence searing into my skin through the layers of cotton. I wet my lips, gazing up at him, noticing his eyes following my actions, red tinging the bottom of his ears.

But then, just as quickly, he paused, his expression changing to one of restraint and propriety.

He withdrew, maintaining a respectable distance between us, and resumed the dance. My mind whirled with disappointment and confusion. Why had he pulled back? Was it hesitation or a matter of propriety? The unanswered questions echoed within me, adding a layer of complexity to the already charged atmosphere.

As the dance came to an end, we both paused, catching our breaths. The unspoken tension lingered between us, the unspoken words hanging in the air. I couldn't help but wonder what could have been, what might have happened if he had chosen to act.

But for now, we remained in the realm of unspoken desires, wrapped in the thrill of a dance that hinted at something more.

8

An Old Gown

I felt guilty as I slipped Leo's mother's gown through my fingers two days later, enjoying the sensation of the smooth fabric against my skin. Even though I should've been trying my hardest to find a way to return to my own time, to my mother, I felt excited at the prospect of attending a ball. And after my practice with Leo, I also craved a repeat of our dance.

The maid, draping the gown over her arm, unfolded it further to show off its splendor. I knew nothing about the fashion of this time so could not tell what was supposed to be old-fashioned about it.

The dress, crafted with meticulous detail, was a stunning representation of the 1700s, to my limited knowledge. Its bodice was adorned with delicate floral embroidery, the threads intertwining to form intricate patterns that shimmered in the soft light. The neckline was modest yet elegant, with a subtle lace trim that added a touch of femininity.

The sleeves were long and fitted, tapering at the wrists before cascading into flared cuffs, embellished with tiny pearl buttons. The fabric itself, a rich satin, was a deep shade of royal blue, as if capturing the essence of the night sky.

I couldn't help but imagine Leo's mother, a woman of elegance and refinement, adorned in this magnificent garment. The thought of wearing it myself felt both thrilling and daunting, as if stepping into the shoes of someone from another era.

As I gazed at the dress, I couldn't help but wonder about the stories it held, the moments it had witnessed.

"I will hang it on your armoire, Miss." The maid retrieved the dress from my grasp, returning it to a hanger and hanging it from the top of the wardrobe in hopes of keeping the fabric wrinkle free. "I shall do your hair and help you dress this Saturday." Her voice betrayed excitement, and she smiled at the dress, patting it one last time before nodding to me.

"Thank you," I told the maid.

As the late afternoon sunlight filtered through the windows of my guest bedroom, casting a warm glow upon the room, there was a soft knock on the door. Startled from my conversation with the maid, I turned to see Amelia standing there, a smile lighting up her face.

"Hello, Rosemary. I've finished all my lessons for the day, and I thought it would be nice to show you something. Come, follow me!"

Curiosity piqued, I nodded and rose from the chair where I had been sitting, leaving the maid to continue her work. Amelia led the way, her small frame practically skipping down the stairs, and I followed closely behind her, eager to see what she had in store.

We stepped outside, and the crisp air enveloped us, carrying with it a faint scent of hay and earth. Amelia guided me towards the stables, her excitement palpable in every step. As we approached, I caught sight of a small, adorable pony nestled in one of the stalls.

"There she is." Amelia's eyes sparkled with affection. "This is Buttercup."

Buttercup, as her name implied, was a sweet and dainty pony, her coat a creamy shade of light brown, adorned with a smattering of white patches resembling delicate buttercup blossoms. Her eyes were gentle and curious, and her mane flowed in untamed waves, kissed by the gentle breeze.

Amelia's voice softened as she opened the stall door. "Buttercup was a gift from my mother. We used to brush her together. She always said that if you own a horse, you should know how to take care of it. It's important to build a bond and trust with them." To hear this ten-year-old girl embody the remnants of a voice much older than she, it tugged at my heartstrings.

Moved by the sentiment and the connection Amelia had with her mother, I smiled and nodded in understanding. "Would you like some help brushing Buttercup?" I didn't want to cross some line, but Amelia seemed eager to share the special bond she had with her mother and it made me wonder if Amelia perhaps missed the company.

Amelia's face lit up with delight. She fetched a couple of brushes, handing one to me. Together, we ran the brushes through Buttercup's silky coat, removing any dirt or tangles with care and precision.

Focused on the work, her gaze resting on Buttercup's hind leg, Amelia opened up further.

"Mother died four years ago. I miss her terribly, but my father doesn't like to talk about her." Amelia continued brushing, though a small tremble in her chin betrayed the emotions coursing through her. "Leo and father argue too much. I don't like it."

"What was your mother's name?" It must have been so difficult for Amelia to lose her mother at only six. I wouldn't know what I'd do if I lost my mother. A pang shot through my heart as I remembered how dire my mother's situation was. If the chemo didn't... No, I couldn't bear to think of that.

"Catherine." Amelia's voice had softened.

"That is a beautiful name."

Buttercup stood patiently, seeming to revel in the attention and affection bestowed upon her, while I listened to everything Amelia remembered about her mother, however small. She seemed lighter once we finished, and glad to have had an attentive listener.

The sun had almost set, disappearing behind the trees in the distance as it cast their silhouettes in pretty reds and oranges while dousing the stables in shadows. We returned the brushes and closed Buttercup's stall after giving the pony a final parting pat on its flank.

"It should be almost dinner time. We should hurry back inside, I imagine your brother and father are waiting for us, wondering where we are."

Amelia nodded and grasped my hand, swinging our arms back and forth as we walked back.

As Amelia and I entered the grand dining room, the air was filled with the clinking of silverware and the bustling movements of maids meticulously arranging the table. Mr. Abernathy, with a stern expression etched on his face, occupied the seat at the head of the table, while Leo, looking distant, sat a few seats away.

The atmosphere in the room tensed, as if an invisible barrier hung between father and son, stifling the warmth that should have existed between them. My gaze shifted between the two, sensing the unspoken conflict that lingered beneath the surface.

Before anyone could exchange pleasantries, Mr. Abernathy turned his attention to Amelia, his voice stern. "Where have you been, Amelia? Running around like that is not proper behavior."

Amelia scurried around the table, avoiding collision with a maid balancing a steaming terrine of soup. Her cheeks flushed with both embarrassment and excitement. "We were at the stables, Father, visiting Buttercup." Her words spilled out in a rush while I took a seat across from Leo.

Leo's eyes sparkled with amusement as he leaned closer to me, his voice low and teasing. "So that's the scent I detect, Rosemary. The fragrance of adventures at the stables." A playful smile danced upon his lips.

I couldn't resist returning his playful banter, a mischievous glimmer in my eyes. "Ah, Leo, you have a keen nose. But I must say, Buttercup is worth smelling bad for." I wiggled my nose at him, trying to hide the smile creeping up my face.

What was it about Leo that made me forget about everything else?

A flicker of surprise crossed Leo's face, as if he hadn't expected me to play along so readily. But he flashed me a roguish grin, most likely thinking of more retorts.

Amelia, oblivious to the underlying dynamics, joined in the lighthearted exchange. "Buttercup is the sweetest pony, Leo! You should come and visit her with us sometime."

Leo's smile widened, his gaze softening as it met mine. "I'd be delighted, Amelia. And perhaps Rosemary can teach us both a thing or two about horsemanship."

"Oh, I doubt that. I've never ridden a horse." I shook my head and laughed as the butler moved in next to me and filled my wine glass. "I'm afraid my encounters with horses this past week have been the extent of my horsemanship."

The servants served the food onto our plates, filling the air with enticing aromas. The dining room table was adorned with an array of delectable dishes, each prepared to satisfy even the most discerning palate.

As we began to savor the flavors of the meal, Mr. Abernathy turned his attention to Amelia, his eyes filled with paternal curiosity. "And how is your piano playing progressing, Amelia?"

I glanced at Amelia, a gentle smile adorning my lips, before addressing Mr. Abernathy. "Amelia has shown remarkable promise, sir. She has been working on her hand positioning, which is essential for developing proper technique." I couldn't keep the hint of pride from my voice. Amelia had been an eager and attentive student.

Mr. Abernathy's stern countenance softened, his eyes

gleaming with approval. "That's good to hear, Rosemary. I have high hopes for Amelia's musical abilities."

Amelia beamed, her face lighting up with pride and excitement. "I've been practicing every day, Father, just like you said."

Leo, sitting beside Amelia, glanced between us. "I'm sure Amelia's progress is thanks to your excellent guidance, Rosemary."

A warmth spread through me at Leo's words, appreciating his recognition of my efforts. "Thank you, Leo. Amelia has been an exceptional student, and it has been a pleasure to witness her growth."

As I savored the various dishes presented before me, my taste buds were treated to the flavors of the 18th century. A succulent roast of tender beef, accompanied by roasted root vegetables and a rich gravy, delighted my palate. The distinct taste of buttery mashed potatoes melted in my mouth, complementing the savory meat. The table was adorned with a selection of seasonal fruits and cheeses, providing a refreshing interlude between bites.

Amidst the delightful indulgence, Leo's voice broke through the lively chatter. "So, Rosemary, did you like the dress?" I caught the mischievous twinkle in his eyes.

I turned to face Leo, a genuine smile gracing my features. "I loved it, Leo. It's a stunning dress, and I'm grateful for the opportunity to wear it to the dance."

Mr. Abernathy, his gaze fixed upon me, joined the conversation. "Rosemary, are you planning to attend the dance at Granhope Manor?"

I nodded, meeting Mr. Abernathy's gaze with a friendly

smile. "Yes, Mr. Abernathy. Leo kindly invited me, and I'm honored to be attending. It will be a wonderful opportunity to experience the festivities."

Leo swallowed a bite of roast and laid down his fork. "Indeed, Father. Rosemary's presence will surely add to the enjoyment of the evening. I invited her myself, and I've taken the liberty of lending her one of Mother's gowns."

Mr. Abernathy nodded. Thankfully, he did not seem to disapprove. "Very well, then. I'm pleased to have you join us, Rosemary. I'm sure the dress will suit you. My wife had excellent taste."

As Amelia dove into one of her stories, distracting Mr. Abernathy, Leo leaned in, a mischievous glint in his eyes. He kept his voice low so he could not be overheard by his father, but for me, they rang clear enough.

"Rosemary, have you always been so skilled at playing the piano, or did you learn to charm the keys just to impress me?"

I smirked, my eyes meeting his with a playful challenge. "Oh, Leo, I must admit, the piano skills were all just an elaborate ploy to capture your attention. It seems to have worked quite well, wouldn't you say?"

Leo, not one to shy away from a clever retort, continued the banter. "Ah, Rosemary, you possess not only musical prowess but also a sharp tongue. I suppose I'm lucky to have found such a captivating companion for the dance."

I tilted my head, a playful grin gracing my lips. "Indeed, Leo. It looks like I'll have to keep you on your toes during the dance, just to ensure you don't become too comfortable."

Amelia, catching the last part of our hushed conversation,

chimed in with a giggle. "Oh, the dance will be the talk of the town. I wish I was old enough to go."

Leo laughed and wrapped an arm around his sister. "That is right, Amelia. But I am certain that Father is relieved to still have a few years left before you go out into society."

9

A Request

Strolling through the grounds the next day, a gentle breeze playing with my curls, I noticed a carriage in the distance making its way toward the estate. Curiosity piqued, I observed as a middle-aged man and a young woman, who appeared to be around my age, stepped out and entered the grand entrance of the mansion. Intrigued but not wanting to intrude, I continued my leisurely walk.

Moments later, a maid approached me, her eyes filled with urgency. She informed me that my presence was requested in the parlor. Concerned, I followed her back inside, my mind racing with questions about the unexpected visitors.

Upon entering the parlor, I found myself face to face with Mr. Abernathy, Leo, the middle-aged man, and the young woman. Mr. Abernathy introduced them as Mr. Ashbrook and his daughter, Miss Ashbrook.

Before I had a chance to utter a word, Mr. Abernathy took

the lead in the conversation. "Rosemary, I apologize for the urgency, but we find ourselves in a bit of a predicament. Mr. Ashbrook here has received news that the musicians he had arranged for the dance have fallen ill and are unable to make it. We need a pianist, and I thought of you."

Mr. Ashbrook nodded in agreement. "Yes, it seems our plans have been derailed. I've heard of your recent appointment as Amelia's piano teacher, and I was wondering if you would be willing to grace us with your musical talent for the dance. We have sent footmen to inquire if there are any local musicians available, but time is of the essence."

I glanced at Leo, who wore a look of hopeful anticipation, and then back at Mr. Ashbrook. "Of course, Mr. Ashbrook, I would be honored to assist. Music is my passion, and I would be delighted to provide the melodies for such a grand occasion."

Mr. Abernathy's face relaxed into a smile, clearly relieved by my willingness to help. "Excellent, Rosemary. I knew we could count on you. We will do our best to find additional musicians, but your contribution will be invaluable."

Mr. Ashbrook pulled sheets of paper from a small case at his feet. "If you would indulge us with a short demonstration, I took the liberty of bringing along the music sheets intended to be played at the dance."

Leo caught my gaze and frowned. "Mr. Abernathy, do you think my father or I would think to hire a piano teacher who did not know what they were doing?"

Leaning forward, Miss Ashbrook picked up her cup of tea and took a small sip before turning her attention to Leo. "My father does not intend to offend you or Mr. Abernathy."

She flashed Mr. Abernathy a disarming smile. "He is merely intent on assuring the dance's success. I am certain you can understand."

"It is not a bother at all." I took the music sheets from Mr. Ashbrook's grip and walked to the pianoforte in the corner, sliding onto the bench.

Sitting in front of the piano, I placed the sheet music onto the stand. The notes and symbols on the pages held the promise of melodies that would soon fill the grand ball-room. I took a moment to absorb this responsibility and the opportunity it presented.

Taking a deep breath, I let my fingers glide over the keys, exploring the different compositions that lay before me. I played snippets from various pieces, showcasing my abilities and attempting to convey the range of emotions and moods that each selection offered. As the music filled the room, I stole glances at Mr. Ashbrook and Miss Ashbrook, hoping to discern their approval.

Their faces lit up with appreciation and delight, and I felt a surge of satisfaction wash over me. It was clear that my performance had appeased their concerns, and I couldn't help but feel a sense of pride at being able to bring them reassurance and joy through my music.

Mr. Ashbrook leaned back in his chair, a contented smile gracing his features. "Rosemary, my dear, your talent is remarkable. I do not doubt that you will do marvelously at the dance. Take the sheet music with you, review it at your leisure, and let the melodies take root in your heart."

I nodded. "Thank you, Mr. Ashbrook. I will devote myself

to perfecting these pieces and ensuring that they enchant all those who attend the dance."

Mr. Ashbrook then turned his attention to the logistics of my arrival at their estate. "Rosemary, shall I arrange for a carriage to pick you up tomorrow?"

Before I could respond, Leo interjected with a charming smile. "No need for that, Mr. Ashbrook. I'll have the honor of escorting Rosemary to your estate myself."

Mr. Ashbrook's eyes twinkled with amusement as he glanced between us. "Ah, Leo, you've taken the initiative. Very well, I trust Rosemary will be in good hands under your escort. We shall eagerly await your arrival tomorrow evening."

With a gracious nod, Mr. Ashbrook and his daughter rose from their seats, bidding us farewell. As they departed, my stomach knotted. The task ahead was both exhilarating and daunting, but with the support and encouragement of those around me, I knew I could rise to the occasion.

***

Anticipation hung heavy in the air as I sat on the edge of my bed, my hands clutching the fabric of my shift. Moonlight spilled through the curtains, casting a soft glow on the worn wooden floor in front of me.

Tomorrow's dance at Granhope Manor loomed before me, and my nerves were in a state of turmoil. Thoughts of my mother, miles and centuries away, plagued my mind. I wondered if she was safe and if she missed me as much as I missed her. And then there was Lyle, my brave brother fighting in the Vietnam War. I whispered a silent prayer, hoping for his safety and yearning for his swift return.

With a sigh that seemed to carry the depth of my worries, I decided to go for a stroll to calm my mind. Slipping out of my bedroom, I descended the stairs with cautious steps, my bare feet gliding over the cold, wooden floors. The parlor beckoned to me, its inviting warmth drawing me in like a comforting embrace.

The room was bathed in the soft glow of the fireplace, its dancing flames casting flickering shadows upon the walls. I tiptoed toward the piano, careful to make no sound that would disturb the tranquility of the night. The ivory keys stood before me like old friends, waiting to be awakened.

Seating myself on the piano bench, I took a deep breath and let my fingers graze the smooth surface. With delicate precision, I began to play the various pieces for the dance, my fingertips gliding across the keys in a dance of their own. Each note resonated through the quiet room, filling the void with melodies of hope and longing.

But as the music swelled and my fingers moved in synchrony, my trance was broken by the sound of approaching footsteps. I ceased playing, my heart skipping a beat, only to find Leo standing at the doorway. I settled back, my shoulders lowering once more. I didn't mind Leo hearing me play.

"Don't stop on my account, Rosemary." Leo hesitated, his figure shrouded in shadows. "I enjoy listening to your music."

I offered him a grateful smile, feeling a wave of warmth spread through me. "Thank you, Leo. I appreciate your kind words, but I assure you, I know these pieces well. I don't need to continue."

Leo took a step forward, his face illuminated by the soft glow of the fire. "Couldn't sleep either?"

I scooted over on the bench, making room for him beside me. "No. Tomorrow's dance has left my mind restless. The music helps me find solace amidst the chaos."

Leo settled next to me, our shoulders touching. The warmth of his presence eased the tension in my body, and together we sat in companionable silence, enveloped by the gentle crackling of the fire.

The worries and uncertainties of the future faded away. Sitting there, the flickering flames casting a mesmerizing dance of light and shadows, a sense of calm washed over me.

Leo's voice broke the silence once more. "I'm glad you're here. It's comforting to know that I'm not the only one grappling with restlessness."

I turned to him, meeting his gaze with a hint of a smile, our shoulders brushing. "Sometimes, it's the quiet moments like these that bring the greatest solace."

I had noticed the strained interactions between Leo and his father. The absence of Leo's mother was a burden that weighed down every member of this family, including Amelia. I did not want to broach a sensitive subject and hurt Leo further, but I thought it was important to share Amelia's words.

"Amelia told me a little bit more about your mother the other day."

I felt Leo stiffen beside me. "Did she now?" He turned his gaze towards me. "What did she say?"

"Amelia misses your mother very much, and she is troubled by the fact that your father does not like to speak about her when she has so very few memories of her mother left. She also doesn't like that you and your father argue often."

"She told you that?" Leo's brow furrowed and his gaze deepened.

I nodded, remaining still beside him, my hands resting in my lap.

Leo sighed. "I've noticed it too. Father rarely mentions her, as if her memory has become too painful for him to bear."

"Losing a loved one is never easy, and grief affects everyone differently. But perhaps Amelia needs some reassurance, a reminder that her mother's memory is still cherished."

"You're right. I'll make sure to talk to Amelia, to share stories and memories of our mother, so she knows how much she meant to us." Leo let out a sad chuckle. "I had no idea she had been paying attention to my interactions with my father. Father and I have always had a complicated relationship, filled with disagreements and clashes of will. It pains me to see Amelia caught in the middle."

I watched Leo, flashing him a reassuring smile. "What happened, if you don't mind me asking?" I squeezed his arm, offering silent support and encouragement.

"I was sixteen when my mother died." Leo's voice was laced with regret. "It was labeled as an accident, a tragic fall from the second-story window. But deep down, I've always wondered if it was something more. If it was a deliberate act."

Leo's confession sent a shiver down my spine, a profound sadness washing over me. His words hung in the air, heavy with vulnerability and pain. The flickering firelight danced across his face, casting a shadow of sorrow that mirrored the depths of his soul. My heart ached for him as he shared his story, revealing a wound that had never truly healed. I could sense the weight of his unanswered questions and the burden he had carried for so long.

I reached out to hold his trembling hand. "Leo, I can't begin to fathom the pain you must have endured, questioning the circumstances surrounding your mother's passing. It's a heavy burden to bear."

He nodded, his eyes reflecting anguish and anger. "And I can't help but blame my father for it. He was consumed by his political pursuits, always prioritizing his position on the board of trade over the well-being of our family. My mother was left alone, confined within the walls of our vast estate."

As Leo's words unfolded, the picture of a fractured family became clearer. I couldn't imagine the isolation his mother must have felt, the loneliness that had become her constant companion. I realized the depth of Leo's pain, the lingering guilt that plagued him.

"Is that why you don't want to join your father on the board of trade?"

"I have to admit it is the main reason."

"You mustn't blame yourself for your mother's passing. It's an unbearable burden to carry, one that no one should bear alone. Sometimes life presents us with circumstances beyond our control, and it's important to remember that your father's choices and your mother's pain were not your responsibility."

Leo's grip tightened on my hand, seeking solace and re-assurance. "I know. But it's hard not to wonder, not to carry this guilt within me. I miss her every day, and the what-ifs consume my thoughts."

I squeezed his hand, offering support in the only way I

knew how. "I can't take away your pain, Leo, but I can be here for you. You don't have to face these emotions alone."

The air crackled with a palpable tension, our shared vulnerabilities lingering between us. Everything shifted, and the connection between Leo and me deepened, taking on a new and undeniable dimension.

I could feel his eyes on me, their intensity burning through the darkness of the room. The vulnerability he had shown, baring his soul and exposing his deepest wounds, had opened a door that neither of us could ignore. It was as if the world around us had faded into insignificance, leaving only Leo and me in this suspended moment.

"Rosemary," Leo whispered, his voice tinged with longing and uncertainty. "I never expected to find someone who could understand me, who could see past the walls I've built. You've become someone... significant to me."

His words hung in the air, and my heart skipped a beat. The realization that he felt a similar connection was both exhilarating and daunting. I wanted to speak, to express the emotions swirling within me, but words failed me.

Instead, I leaned closer, drawn to him by an invisible force. Our breaths mingled, anticipation and desire hanging in the air like a delicate thread. In the soft glow of the fire, I saw a flicker of longing in Leo's eyes, mirrored by my own.

The distance between us grew smaller, our bodies gravitating toward each other as if pulled by an irresistible magnetism. My hand trembled as it reached up to brush against his cheek, feeling the warmth of his skin beneath my fingertips. I traced the lines of his face, the contours of his lips.

Leo's gaze darkened, a seductive sound coming from his

throat as he closed the gap, pressing his lips against mine. He moved tentatively at first, but when I didn't protest, he deepened the kiss, a delicious pressure building inside me. He hooked his arm around me, pulling me flush against his chest.

My right arm trailed up, my hand tangling in his soft, dark hair as he nipped at my jaw. My heart was drumming so loudly that I was surprised Leo had not mentioned it yet.

But I did not want him to stop.

I wanted to lose myself in him.

Leo's hand moved up and down the small of my back, his lips resting against the side of my face. "Rosemary, you are incredible." The words whispered against my ear, sent a shiver down my spine. I moved against him, meeting his lips once more.

Leo tightened his grip around my back and stood from the bench, lifting me on top of the piano. He stood between my thighs, holding me, multiple layers of skirts creating a barrier between us that I was starting to regret.

Drat the fashion of the 1700s.

I wrapped my legs around him, pulling him in as close as I could, the exposed piano keys creating discordant tones as we pressed against them. Our lips clashed as we explored each other. Leo smelled masculine, his scent warm and comforting as it surrounded me. My body lit up at his touch.

I angled my body, breasts pushing up towards him. He trailed his hand down the front of the dress, then, hooking around the hem of the skirt, he moved his fingers against my legs. I shivered as he touched my bare skin, his grip warm as he slowly slid up my calf and along the outside of my thigh.

His fingers pressed into my skin as he continued kissing

me, his breath quickening. I kept my eyes closed, reveling in every sensation. I had friends with boyfriends who had told me what it was like to kiss, but I hadn't. Not until now. Not until Leo.

I completely understood the allure.

My behind on top of the wooden piano, Leo's entire body pressed against me, I had no space to think about anything but what was going on at that moment. How Leo looked and tasted. Where he would touch me next. How my body reacted. It was intoxicating.

My gaze fixated on his striking figure. His dark hair, tousled ever so slightly, framed his face perfectly, accentuating his sharp features. I couldn't help but marvel at his beauty.

Something was captivating about the way his hair fell effortlessly over his forehead, giving him an air of casual charm. It contrasted with his piercing eyes, which held a depth and intensity that drew me in. Whenever our eyes met, it felt as if time stood still, and I found myself lost in the sea of emotions they held.

I couldn't deny the undeniable pull I felt towards him, the way my heart skipped a beat whenever he was near. It was a feeling I couldn't ignore, and I knew deep down that there was something about Leo and the connection we shared.

And he felt the same.

His breath mingled with mine and his lashes brushed my cheek as he deepened his embrace. It felt like we were rushing towards something unspoken. My skin heated underneath his touch; I was glad for the darkened room so Leo could not see my bright red face.

But just as our attachment reached its zenith, a small voice of reason whispered in my ear, reminding me of the delicate circumstances that surrounded us. The dance, the expectations, and the responsibilities that awaited us the next day.

I withdrew, creating a sliver of space between us. It was a bittersweet moment, filled with unspoken longing and uncharted territory. I wanted nothing more than to surrender to the magnetic pull between us, to explore the depths of our desires.

Yet, I knew that rushing into something so profound, so complex, was not the answer. We had only just begun to discover each other's hearts, and we needed to tread carefully to protect the fragile bond we were forging.

Leo's eyes reflected some of my disappointment, a silent acknowledgment of the emotions we both wrestled with. And though a part of me yearned to bridge the gap between us once more, I knew that this was not the time.

With a final glance, filled with a promise of what lay ahead, we slowly parted ways, carrying the weight of unspoken desire and the hope of a future yet to be written. And as I returned to my room, my heart ached with longing and anticipation. I knew that my connection with Leo had the potential to change my life forever.

10

An Indelible Mark

I stepped into my bedroom, closing the door behind me with a soft click. The evening had been filled with a whirlwind of emotions and sensations, and now I found myself seeking solace in the quiet solitude of my own space.

My lips still tingled from the warmth of Leo's kisses, a lingering sensation that sent shivers down my spine. I couldn't help but trace my fingers gently over my lips, reliving the softness of his touch, and the way his lips had moved against mine.

As my fingers brushed against my lips, a blush crept up my cheeks, a visual reminder of the intense emotions that had washed over me. It was desire and longing, a silent plea for more, for the fire that had ignited between us to continue burning.

My hands, now restless, trailed down from my lips, tracing the contours of my body. They lingered on my outer thigh, the place where his hand had gripped my skin, leaving a faint sensation behind. The memory of his hands, strong and gentle, wrapped around me, holding me close, sent a surge of electricity through me once more.

With each passing moment, I felt the intensity of the evening's encounter seep into my very core. The way our bodies had moved together, a perfect harmony of passion and longing, left an indelible mark on my soul. It was a memory I knew I would carry with me, a cherished secret hidden within the depths of my being.

As I peeled off the layers of my dress, allowing it to fall to the ground, I stood there in the soft glow of the candlelight, feeling the cool air caress my exposed skin. I let myself explore the sensation of desire coursing through me, so foreign and new.

With a sigh, I pulled on a shift, the fabric sliding against my skin like a delicate whisper. As I prepared to retire for the night, my thoughts still consumed by the lingering sensations, I couldn't help but wonder what the future held for me.

The events of the past days had been a whirlwind, filled with unexpected encounters, intense emotions, and a growing attraction that I couldn't deny. But amidst the fluttering excitement, a pang of guilt gnawed at the core of my being.

I glanced around the room, my gaze falling on the folded orange shirt and pair of striped pants, reminding me of the life I had left behind. Thoughts of my sick mother, her frail form and tired eyes, flooded my mind, intertwining with the music scholarship I had earned at the prestigious Curtis Institute of Music. The weight of responsibility had always been mine to carry, and it now pressed upon me with an even greater force.

The truth was, being here in this different time, immersed in a world so distant from my own, offered a respite from the overwhelming obligations. In this era, I was free from the constant worry of my mother's health. It was a break from the harsh reality that awaited me upon my return, a temporary escape from the choices I had made to be there for my mother.

But even as I allowed myself a momentary respite, guilt clawed at the corners of my conscience. I questioned whether I had done enough to find a way back, to reunite with my mother, to fulfill my responsibilities. Should I have searched harder for a solution, explored every possible avenue to return to my own time? The answer eluded me, lost in the complexities of this inexplicable journey.

I closed my eyes, taking a deep breath, as if hoping to find clarity within the depths of my being. I couldn't deny the relief I felt in this reprieve. The chance to focus on my passions and desires, to immerse myself in music and indulge in the burgeoning connection with Leo, offered a sense of liberation I hadn't realized I craved.

It was a conflicting realization, an admission that I found solace in the distraction, even if it meant setting aside the weighty responsibilities I carried for a moment. Guilt crashed over me like a wave, but I couldn't deny the truth that whispered in the recesses of my heart—I needed this break, this respite from the burdens that threatened to consume me.

With a heavy sigh, I sat on the edge of the bed, determined to find a balance between the responsibilities of the present and the allure of the past. I knew that my journey was far from over, and I couldn't allow guilt to cloud my judgment or hold me back from embracing the possibilities that lay before me.

The path ahead might be uncertain, and guilt may still linger in the shadows, but I would navigate through it, knowing that my goal remained unchanged—to find my way back home and fulfill the obligations I held dear.

11

A Dance

As the carriage trundled along the winding road toward Granhope Manor, an unspoken tension hung in the air between Leo and me. We exchanged glances, our eyes conveying the longing we felt for each other.

I kept my gaze fixed on the passing scenery outside, my fingers nervously fidgeting with the fabric of my dress. The soft rustle of the carriage and the rhythmic clip-clop of the horses' hooves provided a soothing backdrop, but my heart raced with anticipation.

Glancing over at Leo, I caught him stealing glances in my direction, his eyes lingering just a moment longer than necessary. Our hands brushed as the carriage jostled, sending an electric shock through my veins. We both recoiled, our cheeks flushing.

To anyone else, we appeared as friends, united in our pursuit of music and the impending festivities. But beneath the surface, there was an undeniable magnetism drawing us closer, an unspoken language that spoke volumes in stolen glances and fleeting touches.

I stole a glance at Mr. Abernathy, his attention focused on the passing landscape. It was clear that he remained oblivious to the silent dance of emotions taking place within the confines of the carriage.

I dared to steal another glance at Leo, his features illuminated by the soft glow of the carriage lantern. His eyes held longing and restraint, mirroring my own emotions. We both knew the weight of the unspoken, delicate balance of desire and propriety that we danced upon. The tension between us, while muffled and disguised, fueled the anticipation that swirled within me.

As the carriage approached Granhope Manor, I took a deep breath, attempting to steady the fluttering of my heart. We would play our parts, maintaining decorum in the presence of others, while cherishing the secret bond that bound us together.

With one last stolen glance at Leo, I pushed aside the thoughts of what might come later, focusing on the grandeur and excitement that awaited us at Granhope Manor. This evening would be a delicate dance of emotions, where every step and every touch carried an unspoken meaning. And as the carriage rolled to a stop, I knew that the real journey was only just beginning.

The butler greeted us at the door, his impeccable attire and regal demeanor befitting the occasion. With a bow, he welcomed us inside, and a footman guided me through the opulent halls toward the ballroom.

The soft glow of candlelight bathed the opulent space, casting an ethereal ambiance. I crossed the dance floor, following the footman until standing before me were Mr. Ashbrook and Miss Ashbrook, their anticipation palpable.

Mr. Ashbrook, a distinguished gentleman with salt-and-pepper hair, extended his hand in greeting. "Welcome, Miss Rosemary. We are delighted to have you here tonight."

Beside him stood Miss Ashbrook, a vision of grace and elegance. Her dark curls cascaded down her back, and her eyes sparkled with excitement. She curtsied, acknowledging my presence.

Before I could respond, another figure emerged from the shadows. A refined woman with a kind smile approached us.

Mr. Ashbrook pointed to the woman. "And this is my wife, Mrs. Ashbrook."

I lowered my head briefly. "Pleased to meet you, Mrs. Ashbrook."

"Thank you for joining us, Miss Rosemary. Your talent is appreciated."

I nodded, keeping my posture straightened. "It's an honor to be here, Mrs. Ashbrook. I look forward to playing for the guests tonight."

Mr. Ashbrook interjected, his voice carrying a note of relief. "Indeed, we were fortunate to find a few local musicians to accompany you. They will be playing string instruments, adding to the merriment of the evening."

As the guests began to trickle in, the ballroom came alive with the soft murmur of conversation and the rustle of silk gowns. I found my place at the grand piano, my fingers brushing the keys. It was time to immerse myself in the music, to let the melodies carry me away.

As my gaze swept across the room, it landed on Leo, who stood near the entrance. His eyes locked with mine, and a fire ignited within me. The heat of his approving stare sent a thrill coursing through my veins, mingling with the anticipation of the performance ahead.

With each passing moment, the room filled with an air of anticipation and excitement. The enchanting melodies began to float through the air, carried by the strings of the accompanying musicians. I let my fingers dance across the ivory keys, allowing the music to weave its spell.

As the notes cascaded from my fingertips, filling the grand ballroom, I stole glances at the guests mingling and dancing. Amidst the laughter and swirl of vibrant gowns, I noticed a shift in the atmosphere.

The men from the board of trade had arrived, their presence commanding attention. I watched as they gathered around Mr. Abernathy, engaged in animated conversation. Leo stood by his side, drawn into the discussion. Curiosity sparked within me, wondering what topic had captivated their attention.

But then, my attention was diverted by the arrival of another man. He exuded an air of authority, and the deference with which the others treated him suggested his significance. Was this the elusive Wills Hill that Leo had mentioned?

Lost in my musings, I was startled by Miss Ashbrook's gentle voice at my side. She had approached me, her eyes sparkling with warmth. "Rosemary, you've been playing so wonderfully. If you'd like, you can take a break. The other musicians can continue for a while with only string instruments."

I smiled at her, appreciating the chance to catch my breath amidst the whirlwind of emotions and intrigue. "Thank you, Miss Ashbrook. A short respite would be much appreciated."

Leaving the piano behind for a moment, I followed Miss Ashbrook to a quieter corner of the ballroom. The strains of the music faded into the background as we found a moment of reprieve from the festivities.

As we stood there, I couldn't help but let my gaze wander toward the group of men conversing near Mr. Abernathy. The man who had arrived with an air of authority caught my attention once more, his presence commanding the respect of those around him. Then I watched Leo again, his posture a bit straighter than before, revealing his reluctance to be there with those men.

"I'm sure you would like to greet Mr. Abernathy," Miss Ashbrook said. I agreed. Leo had promised me a dance this evening, and while I was now attending as a musician, I still wanted to make sure he fulfilled his promise

As Miss Ashbrook guided me through the bustling ballroom, we approached the cluster of men where Mr. Abernathy and Leo stood. Mr. Abernathy's eyes lit up as he spotted me, and with his customary grace, he introduced me to the group.

"Gentlemen, may I present Miss Rosemary, our esteemed pianist for this evening."

I nodded politely, acknowledging each of them in turn. Among them stood Wills Hill, the Earl of Hillsborough, the President of the Board of Plantation and Trade; a figure of significance and influence.

His gaze met mine, and curiosity danced in his eyes. "And where might you hail from, my dear? The American colonies, perhaps?"

I smiled, expecting such an inquiry. "Yes, indeed. I moved here seeking better job opportunities."

Leo, quick to interject, chimed in with a touch of admiration in his voice. "And she has succeeded, as you can see."

A momentary pause hung in the air as the earl pondered Leo's words. Then, with a hint of grumbling in his voice, he voiced his thoughts on the rising tensions in the colonies and the growing dissenters who yearned to break free from the British Empire. The other men joined in, their voices adding to the chorus of discontent.

But amidst the fervor, the earl's gaze returned to me, and his tone softened. "Of course, my words do not apply to you, my dear. Working for a man of good character such as Mr. Abernathy, I am certain you are a person of virtue and integrity."

A sense of relief washed over me at his reassurance, even if it carried a subtle undercurrent of the societal judgments that prevailed in this era. I listened, caught between the waves of dissent and the recognition of my place within this complex tapestry of time. In their words and exchanges, I glimpsed the struggles, dreams, and desires of an era on the precipice of change.

As the lively conversations of the men continued, Leo's eyes sought mine, a glimmer of mischief dancing within them. He extended his hand towards me.

"May I have this dance, Miss Rosemary?"

I smiled, feeling a flutter of anticipation in my chest. "I would be delighted."

Before we could make our way to the dance floor, however, the earl interjected with a knowing smile. "Ah, young love. Don't mind us old men and our chatter. Go ahead, dance the night away."

Leo and I exchanged a glance, acknowledging the gentle teasing from the earl. With his permission granted, we found ourselves swept into the rhythm of the music, our bodies moving in synchrony.

As we twirled and swayed amidst the elegance of the ballroom, Leo's eyes never left mine. His voice, soft and intimate, reached my ears over the melodic strains.

"You look beautiful tonight, Rosemary. That dress, my mother's dress, suits you."

A blush crept onto my cheeks, and a playful glint sparked in my eyes. "Well, I must admit, it's quite remarkable what a dress can do. Perhaps I should borrow more of your mother's wardrobe."

Leo chuckled, the sound resonating through our entwined dance. "Careful, Rosemary. I might just start thinking you're trying to steal her style."

Leo's touch sent tingles up my arm, and I couldn't help but let a playful smile escape my lips. "You're quite the dancer, Leo. Did you learn those moves from your father?"

Leo's eyes sparkled with mischief as he twirled me. "Oh, no, Rosemary. My dancing skills are all my own. But I must admit, my father did teach me a thing or two about charm."

I raised an eyebrow. "Is that so? And here I thought charm wasn't something you could teach."

Leo chuckled, his hand resting on the small of my back. "Well, I suppose he did, didn't he? Lucky me."

The music swirled around us, its enchanting melody serving as the backdrop to our playful banter. As we moved together, our bodies brushing against each other with every step, the air crackled with undeniable chemistry.

I leaned in closer, my voice a whisper against his ear. "You know, Leo, I've heard that dancing is like a conversation without words. What do you think we're saying to each other right now?"

Leo's gaze locked with mine, his smile turning mischievous. "I think we're saying that words aren't necessary when our bodies can do all the talking."

A blush spread across my cheeks, but I couldn't deny the thrill that surged through me at his words. The dance continued, our playful banter turning into a dance of flirtatious glances and subtle touches.

As the song drew to a close, Leo dipped me low, his eyes never leaving mine. "You know, Rosemary, they say the best dancers share a deep connection. I think we've just proven them right."

I laughed, my heart fluttering. "I suppose we have. But the night is still young, Leo. Who knows what other connections we might discover?"

Leo's smile widened, his eyes sparkling with a newfound intensity. "I look forward to finding out, Rosemary. Shall we continue this dance, or shall we explore what else the night has in store for us?"

The playful banter between us continued, filled with laughter and teasing, each word laced with the undeniable undercurrent of romantic tension that had been building between us. It felt as though the world around us faded into the background, leaving only the two of us dancing in a realm of our own.

But like all dances, ours eventually came to an end. With a final twirl and a lingering touch, Leo guided me back towards the piano where I belonged, returning to his father's side.

As I settled back into the familiar position, my fingers once again gliding over the keys, Leo's presence lingered in my thoughts. The melodies I played carried echoes of our dance, intertwined with the whispers of his voice and the warmth of his touch.

And as the piano music filled the ballroom once more, I couldn't help but steal a glance in Leo's direction, a smile playing at the corners of my lips. The night was far from over, and I knew that in this enchanting world of swirling emotions and stolen moments, anything was possible.

12

An Accusation

As the evening wore on and the dance reached its final moments, I decided to relinquish the piano to the skilled string musicians. The soft melodies continued to weave through the ballroom, but my focus had shifted to finding Leo once more, eager for another opportunity to speak with him and perhaps share another dance before the night's end.

Scanning the ballroom, my eyes searched for his familiar face or the distinct figure of Mr. Abernathy. However, amidst the mingling guests, they were nowhere to be found. A flicker of concern danced within me, urging me to seek them out.

Leaving the ballroom behind, I ventured down an empty hallway, the soft glow of the chandeliers casting a warm, inviting light. The distant murmur of voices reached my ears, drawing my attention. Could it be Leo? Was he the source of those hushed conversations?

My steps quickened as curiosity and anticipation intertwined. I followed the sound, my heart pounding in anticipation with each passing moment.

As I stood outside the room, the hushed voices grew clearer. My heart quickened, realizing that I had stumbled upon a private conversation. Unable to resist my curiosity, I pressed my ear against the door, straining to hear the words being exchanged inside.

"The taxation plans must be executed swiftly and effectively," a deep voice declared with an air of authority. "We cannot allow the colonies to think they can challenge the British rule."

Another voice, more measured and calm, chimed in. "Yes, indeed. And we must focus on dismantling the factions that seek to disrupt our unity. We need to show them the consequences of rebellion."

My mind raced as I recognized the voices. It was Mr. Abernathy and Wills Hill, along with a few others whose names I didn't catch. The conversation centered on suppressing the growing dissent in the American colonies and tightening control over trade and taxation.

I listened, and my breath caught in my throat. I read about what they were discussing in school books. How could I have stumbled upon such a clandestine discussion?

As their voices faded, I gathered the courage to inch closer to the door, desperate to catch every word. They spoke of strategies to cripple the economy, discussing trade restrictions and ways to weaken the dissenting factions. It became clear that they saw these measures as necessary to maintain control over the colonies.

My mind raced; Leo could be inside that room, but I

should not be here. I couldn't ignore the danger of being discovered eavesdropping.

Taking a deep breath, I backed away from the door. Perhaps Leo was in a different part of Granhope Manor; I should return to the ballroom to see if I had missed him.

A strong grip tightened around my shoulder, halting my movements. My heart raced as I turned to face one of the men from the board of trade. His eyes bore into mine with amusement and suspicion.

"Well, well, what do we have here? Caught in the act of eavesdropping, were we?"

A surge of panic shot through me, and I stammered, attempting to explain myself. "No, sir, I was just... I was on my way back to the ballroom. I wasn't eavesdropping, I swear!"

But my pleas fell on deaf ears as the man opened the door to the room and pushed me inside. The other men turned their attention toward me, their gazes filled with scrutiny and skepticism.

"Look who I found lurking outside." Smug satisfaction laced his voice. "A spy, perhaps?"

The room fell into an uncomfortable silence, and all eyes focused on me, waiting for an explanation. Wills Hill rose from his seat, his piercing gaze fixed upon me.

"And who are you, Miss..." The earl's voice trailed off, his words laced with suspicion.

"I-I'm Rosemary. We met earlier in the ballroom. I was... I was only looking for Leo. I didn't mean to intrude."

Wills Hill's expression remained stern; his eyes narrowed as he continued to interrogate me. "Coincidence seems to favor you a little too much, don't you think? A girl from the colonies just happens to appear outside Mr. Abernathy's estate and finds herself conveniently invited in. And now, here you are, attempting to listen in on our conversation."

Mr. Abernathy's voice rose in defense of me. "Now, now, sir, let us not jump to conclusions. Rosemary has been a guest at my estate, invited by Leo. Perhaps she is simply searching for him, as she claims."

But the earl remained resolute, dismissing Mr. Abernathy's defense. "It's curious, isn't it? The original musicians fall ill, and suddenly Rosemary steps in to fill the void. It provides her with the perfect opportunity to be here and listen to our discussions."

Desperation tinged my voice as I tried to explain. "I assure you, I do not know why the musicians have fallen ill. Leo invited me to the dance, and I accepted. I am not a spy."

The earl's skepticism did not waver, and the other men nodded in agreement, their suspicion evident. The tension in the room tightened like a vise, suffocating any hope of vindication.

Faced with their collective skepticism, I felt my heart sink. Their accusations bore down upon me, threatening to crush the truth that burned within my chest. I searched their faces, desperate for any sign of belief, but all I found was a sea of distrust.

Fear gripped me as their suspicion pressed down upon me, threatening to smother any hope of escape. The earl's intense gaze bore into my soul.

"We can't let her go. We must consider the possibility that she is a spy sent here to gather information on our plans."

The other men nodded in agreement, their eyes filled with

suspicion. Panic surged through my veins, but I fought to maintain my composure, refusing to let them see my fear.

Mr. Abernathy, who had been the voice of reason, interjected. "Gentlemen, let us not rush to judgment. While we must exercise caution, we should also consider the possibility that Rosemary's presence here is coincidental."

The earl's eyes narrowed, his voice dripping with doubt. "Coincidence upon coincidence, Abernathy? It stretches the limits of plausibility."

Sweat trickled down my brow as I searched for a way to prove my innocence. "I swear, I am not a spy. I do not know your plans or your discussions. I came here tonight to enjoy the dance, to spend time with Leo."

A flicker of doubt crossed Mr. Abernathy's face, but the others remained unconvinced. Their collective suspicion threatened to crush me under immense pressure.

After a brief exchange of whispers, one of the men suggested contacting the authorities, ensuring a thorough investigation. Panic surged through me at the thought of being imprisoned, my life torn apart by false accusations. What would happen to me then? Would I ever find my way back to my own time?

Mr. Abernathy's voice rose once again, attempting to find a compromise. "Instead of involving the authorities, why don't we exercise caution and put Rosemary on house arrest? We can confine her to the guest room in my home while we investigate her claims further."

The suggestion hung in the air, and the room filled with a heavy silence. I glanced between the men, desperation etched upon my face. Every fiber of my being resisted the idea of being locked away, cut off from the world, and trapped in a web of suspicion.

The earl's gaze bore into mine; his voice laced with suspicion. "And what guarantee do we have that she won't attempt to escape, to flee and bring danger upon us?"

Mr. Abernathy's voice held a touch of empathy as he addressed the earl's concern. "We can assign a guard to watch over her, ensuring she remains within the confines of the guest room. It will give us time to investigate her claims while preventing any potential harm."

My heart pounded as their words settled upon me, the reality of the situation sinking in. I had become entangled in a web of intrigue and suspicion, and now I faced the prospect of confinement within the very house that had initially offered solace and escape.

As their discussions continued, my mind raced, searching for a way to prove my innocence and regain my freedom. The clock ticked away, each passing second intensifying the knot of fear that twisted within me.

My heart sank as Mr. Abernathy and the earl took hold of my arms, their grip firm and unyielding. We began to make our way down the hallway, their intentions clear; to transport me to Mr. Abernathy's estate and confine me to a guest room. Desperation welled within me, fueling my determination to find a way out of this dire situation.

As we moved, their presence and the impending imprisonment settled upon me like a heavy shroud. Fear mingled with anger, creating a turbulent storm within my chest. I searched for hope, a chance to convince them of my innocence.

Midway down the hallway, my heart skipped a beat as Leo

emerged from the ballroom, his eyes widening in shock at the sight of Mr. Abernathy, the earl, and me. He quickened his pace, his voice filled with concern and defiance.

"What in the world is happening here? Father, why are you manhandling Rosemary like this?"

Mr. Abernathy's face hardened, his gaze unwavering. "Leo, this is not the time. There are matters at hand that require resolution, and unfortunately, Rosemary has become entangled in them."

Leo's eyes darted between his father and me, confusion and anger flickering across his features. "But whatever you think she's done, I trust that she's innocent! You can't just lock her up without any evidence or proper investigation. This isn't right!"

The earl, asserting his authority, stepped forward, his tone stern and commanding. "I understand your concern, Leo, but we cannot afford to take any chances. The tensions are escalating, and we must act to protect our interests. Rosemary will be placed under house arrest at Mr. Abernathy's estate until the situation can be resolved."

Leo's jaw clenched, his voice tinged with frustration. "There has to be another way, Father. We can't condemn an innocent person based on mere suspicions."

Mr. Abernathy's expression softened, his voice filled with regret. "I wish there were, my son, but the stakes are too high. We must do what we believe is necessary to quell the tensions and protect what we care about."

Leo, his eyes filled with determination and concern, turned to me. "Rosemary, I won't let them lock you away. I'll find a way to help you, I promise."

His words ignited a flicker of hope within me, a spark that refused to be extinguished.

A heavy sigh escaped Mr. Abernathy's lips, and he cast a weary gaze upon his son. "Leo, I understand your concerns, but I need you to trust me on this. We have important matters to attend to, and it's best if you go and thank Mr. and Mrs. Ashbrook for their hospitality. Meet us back at home later."

Leo's eyes darted back and forth between his father and me, frustration and determination etched on his face. He nodded, his voice tinged with lingering worry. "All right, Father. But I won't rest until we find a way to prove Rosemary's innocence."

With those words hanging in the air, Leo turned on his heel and walked away, his figure slowly receding into the distance. The ache of his absence swelled within me, but I knew that his promise would be my beacon of hope in the days to come.

Left alone with Mr. Abernathy and the earl, I felt a wave of apprehension wash over me. The gravity of my situation settled upon my shoulders as we approached Mr. Abernathy's awaiting carriage. The ride back to Mr. Abernathy's estate was filled with an oppressive silence, each passing mile a reminder of the uncertain future that awaited me.

I stole glances at Mr. Abernathy and the earl, their expressions resolute and unyielding. Their authority bore down upon me, making it clear that escape would not come easily. My mind raced, searching for any possible means of vindication and release from the confines of house arrest.

As the carriage came to a halt, my heart sank at the sight of Mr. Abernathy's estate looming before us. The familiar grandeur of the mansion now felt like a foreboding prison, its walls closing in around me.

Stepping out of the carriage, I found myself flanked by Mr. Abernathy and the earl, their presence a constant reminder of my precarious situation.

Together, we made our way toward the entrance, the door opening to reveal the opulent interior. The hushed whispers of the other men mingled with the sound of our footsteps, a chorus of uncertainty and speculation that hung heavy in the air.

13

House Arrest

I sat on the edge of the bed, my heart pounding in my chest as I listened to the muffled sounds beyond the door. The constant shuffling of footsteps and the occasional creak of the floorboards were a constant reminder of my captivity.

My body had felt so wired, my mind racing with thoughts that I had hardly been able to sleep last night. Exhaustion settled in my bones and made my nerves stretch thin.

Restlessness gnawed at me, the walls of the guest room closing in with each passing moment. How was I supposed to find a way back to my own time, to my mother, when I was locked away in this room? My fingers clenched into tight fists, frustration surging through my veins. I longed for the freedom to roam, to explore every avenue that might lead me to the answers I sought.

The sound of the doorknob turning broke through the silence, and my heart skipped a beat. Swinging the door open, a maid entered, carrying a tray topped with food and a steaming pot of tea. She placed it on a small side table with a gentle smile before exiting, leaving me alone with my thoughts once again.

I eyed the tray, the aroma of the food wafting through the air. Hunger gnawed at my stomach, but my appetite waned in the face of my current predicament. The meal before me felt like an offering meant to keep me complacent, a subtle reminder of the power others held over my fate.

I reached for the teapot and poured myself a cup, the warmth seeping into my hands as I cradled it. The fragrant steam rose, soothing my troubled mind. Sipping the tea, I allowed its comforting taste to distract me from the uncertainty that loomed.

But even in this momentary break, the questions persisted. What would become of me? Would I be forever confined within these walls, my existence reduced to a mere pawn in a game I barely understood? Would Leo come for me?

As I took another sip of tea, determination resurfaced. I couldn't surrender to despair, not when there was still a possibility. I would persevere, against all odds, for the sake of my freedom and the chance to return to the life I left behind.

***

The time passed without incident though I was bored out of my mind staring at the same wallpaper all day. Perhaps no one was coming to see me today. Judging by the dark sky outside, it was getting late. I doubted that any of the men from the board of trade would disturb me now. I might as well prepare myself for sleep.

Sitting at the vanity, I wet my face with a cloth and released my hair, letting the curls sweep along my shoulders.

The door to my guest room creaked open. I stood, my eyes wide with apprehension. Who could be entering my room at this late hour? But before I could utter a word, a hushed voice reached my ears, urging me to be quiet.

It was Leo. He had somehow managed to sneak past the guard posted outside my door.

"How?" I muttered under my breath. I remained still, staring at him.

Leo moved into the room. The dim light from the hallway illuminated his face, revealing a mischievous glint in his eyes. Without a word, he closed the door behind him, as if sealing us away from the outside world.

I couldn't help but take a step closer, my heart pounding. The weight of the day's confinement lifted as Leo approached me, his arms outstretched. Everything else faded away, and all that mattered was the connection between us.

With an almost instinctual understanding, I moved into his embrace, feeling the warmth of his body against mine. It was a silent reassurance, a shared solace in a time of uncertainty. He held me as if he was afraid I would be torn away from him.

"We'll have to be quiet," Leo whispered in my ear. "Gabriel Sullivan—your guard—fell asleep. I don't know how long he'll be out."

I fisted the shirt fabric on his back, glad to have Leo near me again.

I could feel the intensity of Leo's embrace deepening, drawing me closer to him, as if he wanted to merge our very souls. His darkening gaze reminded me of the other day in the parlor. The air between us crackled. Time stood still as our bodies pressed against each other, a magnetic pull that defied the boundaries of reason.

Our hearts beat in synchrony, as if composing a symphony of unspoken words. His touch sent shivers down my spine, igniting a fire within me that I had never experienced before. The tension between us was palpable, a delicate dance between temptation and restraint.

I could see a reflection of my longing mirrored in his gaze. It was as if the world around us had faded into insignificance, leaving only the two of us. The sight of him warmed my heart and eased the tension in my tired body. Every brush of his fingers against my skin, every shared breath, spoke volumes, filling the silence with a language that only we understood.

I felt alive, electrified by the connection we shared. It was as if the struggles of our circumstances dissolved, and for a fleeting moment, there was only the undeniable chemistry between us.

But as quickly as the moment had arrived, it dissipated, leaving a lingering ache in my heart. Leo released his grip, allowing space to form between us. His eyes held a mixture of longing and resignation, mirroring the turmoil that swirled within my own heart.

Leo's voice, soft yet filled with determination, broke the silence. "I couldn't stand the thought of you being locked away like this, Rosemary. I had to see you, to make sure you were all right."

I nodded against his chest, my voice less than a whisper. "I've been so worried, Leo. Locked in here, not knowing what would happen next... But seeing you here, with me, gives me hope."

He held me tighter, as if protecting me from the accusations that had put me under house arrest. "I won't let anything happen to you, Rosemary. I'll find a way to keep you safe, to uncover the truth behind all of this."

With Leo by my side, I felt stronger, more secure, and capable to withstand whatever was coming my way. The worries and doubts that had plagued me throughout the day faded into the background, replaced by a sense of hope.

With a bittersweet smile, I finally pulled away, reluctantly releasing myself from his embrace. "Thank you for coming, Leo. I don't know what I would do without you."

Leo's gaze locked with mine, a tender expression adorning his features. "We'll find a way, Rosemary. I promise. But for now, you should get some rest. We'll face whatever comes our way together."

As I watched him retreat toward the door, I couldn't help but feel a pang of longing. But I knew that he couldn't stay. If he did, he would be caught as well.

With a final lingering glance, Leo stepped back, disappearing into the shadows. I watched him close the door, a knot forming in the pit of my stomach. The ache of longing remained, but so did the fierce determination to find a way out of my house arrest. I crawled underneath the bed cover and let myself drift off to sleep.

****

I woke from my sleep, slowly emerging from the depths of my dreams as the sound of raised voices pierced through the morning quietude. As consciousness returned, I recognized Mr. Abernathy and Leo's familiar voices engaged in a heated argument. My heart quickened with curiosity and concern about the reason for their argument.

Their voices carried through the walls, their words laced with tension and resentment. Leo's voice rose above the rest, filled with a raw emotion that I had not heard before.

"You care more about your ambitions than you do about your own family!" Leo's voice echoed through the air, trembling with hurt. "You were never there for us...for Mother."

A heavy silence hung in the air, pregnant with unspoken truths. I strained to listen, my heart aching for Leo's pain. The accusations flew back and forth, a whirlwind of pent-up emotions unleashed.

Then, Leo's voice cracked, filled with a sorrow that cut through the tension. "Amelia hardly remembers our mother. She wanted to know more about her, about the woman who gave her life. But you were absent, consumed by your work. You did not want us to speak about her. I blame myself too for not seeing it. Amelia told Rosemary, but she should have felt comfortable enough to speak with me, her brother."

My breath caught in my throat, the revelation striking me like a bolt of lightning. Leo had bared his soul, revealing the wounds that had festered beneath the surface for far too long. His words hung in the air, heavy with regret and the unspoken yearning for a connection that had been denied.

I remained frozen on the bed, my heart breaking for Leo

and the fractured relationship he shared with his father. It was a moment of vulnerability and truth, a glimpse into the depths of their family dynamics.

Listening, I realized the profound impact that Leo's words held. They were an expression of a deep longing for love and understanding, a plea for his father to prioritize the relationships that mattered. The raw honesty in Leo's voice resonated within me, the weight of his pain etching itself into my soul.

The tension hung thick in the air, each word uttered a sharp dagger that pierced my heart. But amidst the turmoil, hope emerged.

Leo's voice rose above the fray. "I've come to check on Rosemary and bring her something to eat."

"Son..." Mr. Abernathy sighed. He sounded weary, defeated. "All right. We'll continue this conversation later."

As their voices grew closer, anticipation pressed upon me. The door creaked open, and there stood Leo, holding a tray laden with food. His eyes met mine, filled with concern and determination.

"Rosemary, how are you? Have you managed to sleep?" He flashed a smile though I could tell he was still pained from the argument with his father.

I smiled back, offering reassurance. "I'm holding up, Leo. Thank you for coming and for bringing me breakfast."

He placed the tray on the nearby table, his eyes never leaving mine. With a tenderness that both soothed and ignited my heart, he took my hand in his. "I won't let this situation persist, Rosemary. I promise you that I'll find a way to set things right."

Leo had a magical way with words that made me believe

everything he said. If he assured me that he would find a way, then I would have to trust that he would.

Leaning closer, Leo's gaze held mine, his eyes filled with an intensity that sent a shiver down my spine. "You're not alone in this, Rosemary."

His words were like a balm to my wounded soul, their meaning resonating deeply within me. It was strange how fast a connection had formed between us; it defied circumstance and reason. Part of me had to admit that being around Leo made me want to forget about my own time and troubles.

I squeezed Leo's hand. "Thank you." He nodded, a silent agreement passing between us.

As Leo withdrew his hand, his touch lingering for a moment, he offered a gentle smile. "Take care, Rosemary. I'll be back soon. Stay strong."

His departing words echoed in the room, leaving behind a sense of warmth and reassurance. I watched him leave, his figure receding down the hallway, and I clung to the belief that with his support, I would find a way out of this.

14

An Investigation

My heart pounded with anticipation and trepidation as I followed the guard's lead. It had been days since I had seen Leo, and this was the first time I was asked to leave the guest room. We walked down the familiar hallways, the weight of my confinement heavy on my shoulders. As we approached the parlor, I could hear murmurs and the shuffling of papers from within, hinting at a group of people gathered together.

The door swung open, and I stepped into the room, my gaze sweeping across the faces of those present. The Earl of Hillsborough, Mr. Abernathy, and several other men from the board of trade stared back at me, their expressions a blend of curiosity and suspicion. But it was Leo's presence that anchored me, his steady gaze offering reassurance amidst the uncertainty.

"What is going on?" I shifted my weight as I stood staring at the men, the guard by my side.

Leo stepped forward, raising his voice to be heard by the crowd. "We have been conducting an investigation, Rosemary." His eyes met mine; he nodded in assurance. "I could not bear the thought of you being wrongfully accused, so I took it upon myself to gather evidence of your innocence."

His words sank into the room, silence enveloping us as all eyes turned to Leo. He produced a stack of documents from a nearby table, compiled evidence that represented his tireless efforts these past few days.

Leo's gaze shifted from the papers to the gathered men, his voice strong and unwavering. "Gentlemen, what you thought to be true about Rosemary was based on assumptions and misguided suspicions. I have spent days gathering evidence, speaking to witnesses, and verifying her character."

He began to present his findings, one by one, the weight of his words resonating through the room. Each document and testimonial spoke in defense of my innocence, unraveling the doubts that had plagued my presence among them.

I was honestly surprised by Leo's meticulous research since I had doubts that there was anything to prove my innocence. Traveling through time did not leave a person with many leads to follow.

Leo's voice resonated with conviction as he spoke, his eyes meeting the skeptical gazes of the men before him. "Gentlemen, I have thoroughly investigated the claims against Rosemary, and I am here to present irrefutable evidence that disproves any notion of her involvement or wrongdoing."

He held up the first document, a detailed account of the events surrounding the supposed illness of the original musicians. "Here is the truth about the musicians. Contrary to what was believed, they were not tampered with or coerced. They chose to indulge in revelry and, as a result, were too intoxicated to fulfill their commitment."

A murmur rippled through the room as the realization sank in. The foundation upon which the accusations against me had been built was crumbling, replaced by the truth that Leo had unearthed.

Leo continued, his gaze unwavering, as he spoke of my character and integrity. "Rosemary has never shown any interest in prying into my father's work or influencing my decisions regarding the Board of Trade. She has respected our boundaries and supported my pursuits without ulterior motives."

Leo then produced a written statement from Miss Ashbrook, her words a powerful testament as well. He held up another paper. "Here is a statement from Miss Ashbrook herself. She declares that Rosemary approached her about seeking my whereabouts, appearing in that hallway by pure chance and not with any malicious intent."

The room fell into a heavy silence, the evidence leaving little room for doubt. I felt my breath catch, my eyes locked on Leo; he seemed so confident and self-assured.

I stepped forward, finding my voice amidst the lingering echoes of doubt. "Gentlemen, I assure you, my intentions have always been pure. I came here seeking a new opportunity, a chance to prove myself and contribute to this community. I never meant any harm or wished to undermine anyone's trust."

Leo took my hand in his as I spoke, his touch providing an

anchor of support and assurance. Together, we stood united, determined to unveil the truth and restore my reputation.

The air in the room shifted, skepticism melting away as the evidence settled upon the hearts of those present. Their glances shifted from doubt to acknowledgment, from suspicion to understanding.

Leo's voice cut through the silence once more. "Let us set aside misguided judgments and embrace the truth." His gaze swept across the room. "Rosemary's innocence has been proven beyond doubt. It is time we extend her the respect and trust she deserves."

A wave of agreement washed over the room, the tension dissolving as the men acknowledged their misconceptions and the need for redemption. They offered their apologies, their words a balm to my wounded spirit.

Mr. Abernathy's face shifted from skepticism to astonishment, his eyes widening as the truth unfolded before him. His gaze met mine, and in that fleeting moment, I saw a flicker of remorse and regret.

I turned to Leo, my heart fluttering with relief. My voice choked with emotion. "Leo, you did all this for me?"

He nodded, a smile playing at the corners of his lips. "I couldn't bear to see you suffer, Rosemary. You deserve better than that."

Surrounded by the evidence of Leo's unwavering support and the newfound understanding among the men, I felt a weight lift from my shoulders. As the room began to disperse, the tension replaced by a sense of relief, I took Leo's hand in mine, squeezing it.

With gratitude in my heart, I whispered, "Thank you, Leo, for believing in me."

His grip tightened, his eyes reflecting a depth of emotion that mirrored my own. "Always, Rosemary." I savored the warmth of his hand. "Always."

As Leo guided me back to the guest room, my heart swirled. The weight of the past days lifted from my shoulders. We stepped inside the room, the door closing behind us, and for a moment, we stood in the tranquil space, the only sound the soft rustling of our breaths.

Leo turned to face me, his eyes filled with kindness and something else—something that made my heart skip a beat. "Rosemary, I cannot express how relieved I am that this matter has been resolved. I never doubted your innocence for a moment, and I am sorry for the trouble my family has put you through."

I nodded, my own emotions threatening to spill over. The magnitude of the moment hung in the air, and I could sense that there was more Leo wanted to say.

His gaze locked with mine. "Rosemary, throughout these events, I've come to realize something profound. Despite the turmoil, being by your side has brought me a sense of solace, strength, and joy that I have rarely experienced before."

My heart raced as I absorbed his words, realizing the depth of his feelings. His next words carried a vulnerability that pierced through any remaining doubt. "Rosemary, I love you. I wish for nothing more than to explore the connection between us, to see where it might lead."

I felt a rush of warmth envelop me, my feelings rising to the surface. His declaration resonated deep within me, awakening a longing I had not dared to contemplate. I admired Leo's kindness, intelligence, and unwavering support. And now, with his heartfelt confession, I couldn't deny the blossoming love within my own heart.

A smile tugged at the corners of my lips as I stepped closer to Leo. "Leo, I, too, have felt a connection between us. Despite the trials we've faced, being with you has brought me happiness and a sense of belonging I never thought possible."

I reached out, my hand finding its way to his, our fingers intertwining, creating a bond that felt both delicate and unbreakable. "I would be honored to explore this relationship with you, to face whatever challenges may come our way, together." My mind drifted to my family. Could I truly remain here and not find a way to travel back to my own time?

Leo kissed me, his eyes closing as he held me tight. When he broke free, he sighed. "Promise me, we'll continue this later." He sounded wistful as he gazed into my eyes.

I nodded.

"Good." He smiled, lifting my hand and kissing the top of my fingers. "I will finish up everything with the board of trade, so take some time to prepare yourself and meet me in the back garden in... let's say an hour?"

"I promise."

***

I braided my hair, weaving the strands together, and applied a touch of scented balm on my wrists and neck, cherishing the sweet fragrance that lingered in the air. With anticipation coursing through my veins, I made my way to the back garden, where I hoped to find Leo waiting. The thought of his warm embrace ignited a flutter in my heart.

As I stepped outside, the gentle breeze caressed my cheeks, and the soft rustling of leaves whispered in my ears. However, my attention quickly shifted as I caught the sound of Mr. Abernathy's voice, carrying a tone of genuine remorse. Curiosity piqued, I quietly approached the spot where their conversation unfolded, hidden from view by the decorative bushes.

Mr. Abernathy's voice trembled as he spoke to Leo, his words carrying a weight that mirrored the depth of his regret. "Leo, my son. I want to apologize. I should have talked to you about your mother, about her struggles with her mental health. I failed to provide the support she needed, and I let Amelia slowly forget the memory of her mother."

My heart ached at the raw vulnerability in Mr. Abernathy's voice, and I couldn't help but pause, allowing their words to weave through the air. I could not interrupt their conversation now. This was something Leo had needed for a long time.

Mr. Abernathy continued, his voice tinged with remorse and love. He shared the story of his relationship with Leo's mother, illuminating the complexities they faced. He confessed his deep affection for her, tempered by the challenges that her mental health brought.

"Leo, I wanted your mother, you, and Amelia to be with me in London. But she refused, and in hindsight, I realize that I should have never left you and your sister behind to shoulder the burden of her care."

Leo's voice, laden with emotion, broke through the air as

he asked the question that weighed on his heart. "Father, why would you leave us to deal with this on our own? Why did you choose work over your own family?"

"My son, I cannot undo the choices I made. I can only express my deepest apologies for the pain and burden I placed upon you and Amelia. You both mean the world to me, and I will spend the rest of my days making amends, cherishing the bond we have as a family."

Tears welled up in my eyes as I listened to their conversation, witnessing the depth of their shared history, and the tangled web of love, sacrifice, and regret that entwined their lives.

I stood in the garden, contemplating the moment I had just witnessed between Mr. Abernathy and Leo, when a presence materialized beside me. My gaze shifted to the woman who appeared to be in her early thirties, an air of mystique surrounded her. Then I noticed her clothing, which was very out of place for this era but would fit in perfectly in my own time.

I regarded her with suspicion. "Who are you? What is your purpose here?"

The woman's lips curled into a gentle smile as she met my gaze. "I am the caretaker of the bookshop that transported you to this moment, Rosemary. I have been watching over you, and now, I have come to present you with a choice."

"A choice?" Somehow her words sent anticipation and trepidation coursing through me.

The woman continued, her words hanging in the air like an unspoken promise. "You have the power to decide whether to stay in this time, allowing your love for Leo to bloom further, or return to your own time, to the family you hold dear."

Her words struck a chord within me, resonating with the echoes of Mr. Abernathy and Leo's conversation about the importance of family. My heart felt heavy as I thought of my sick mother, confined to her bed, and my brother, serving in a distant land.

Tears spilled over, and it felt like my heart was caught in a vice. "I love Leo with all my heart, but I cannot forsake my own family. My mother needs me, and my brother... He is fighting a war. I cannot abandon them. Is there no other way? Can I not return to Leo later?

The woman shook her head. "This is a one-time offer."

"Can I have more time? Please, I can't leave him without an explanation. Surely there's time for me to write a letter?"

"I am sorry, dear. But it is now or never. What will your decision be?"

My heart felt torn, yearning to stay and explore the depths of my connection with Leo, yet recognizing the sense of duty that tugged at my soul. I knew that my presence in this time, however captivating and wondrous, was but a fleeting chapter in the grand tapestry of my life.

With a heavy sigh, I mustered the strength to speak the words that echoed within my heart, a bittersweet melody of longing and sacrifice. Leo would be all right without me. "I choose to return to my own time, to my family."

My heart clenched as I gave my answer to the strange woman. I understood that my journey had reached its end and that the bonds I had forged in this past era would forever remain etched in my heart. I could not face Leo and tell him that I was leaving; I could only hope that he would forgive me and, in time, think fondly of me.

The woman nodded, her gaze warm and understanding. "Your decision comes from a place of love and responsibility, Rosemary. It is not an easy choice, but it is a noble one."

With a final glance back at the garden, where the faint echo of love's possibility lingered, I prepared myself for the return to my own time—a world far removed from the antiquated beauty of 1764.

15

A Choice

As I stepped back into my own time, the world around me seemed unchanged, as if no time had passed at all. Yet, in my hands, I clutched a small green book—a tangible reminder of the extraordinary journey I had just embarked upon. The fabric of the old-fashioned dress clung to my body, serving as a silent testament to the reality of my time-traveling escapade.

What had I been doing in town when I disappeared? My mind raced past all the time I had spent at Leo's estate, rewinding my memories until I remembered. I had been picking up my mother's medication. No, I was still picking up mother's medication.

Making my way to the town's pharmacy, I entered with a sense of both apprehension and relief. The pharmacist, Mr. Jenkins, a kind-hearted man with thinning gray hair, glanced up from behind the counter and raised an eyebrow at my attire.

"Well, well, someone's gone all out for a costume party, I see." He chuckled, laughing at his joke. "Done some shopping for an event?"

I managed a small smile, the lie weighing upon me. "Yes, indeed. It will be quite the party. I wanted to make sure I looked the part."

The pharmacist nodded, accepting my explanation without further inquiry. He handed me the medication I had come for, his gaze lingering on my face for a moment before returning to his work.

Leaving the pharmacy, I made my way back home, feeling exhaustion and gratitude for the return to the familiar. As I stepped through the front door, I shed the old-fashioned dress like a discarded cocoon, grateful to slip back into the comfort of my clothes.

With renewed purpose, I ventured further into the house, seeking out the sanctuary of my mother's presence. I found her in the living room, her frail figure nestled in an armchair, surrounded by the remnants of a life interrupted by illness.

Setting the glass of water and the prescribed medication on the nearby table, I approached her with a gentle smile. "Hello, Mom."

Her eyes met mine, tired yet filled with recognition. "Rosemary, my dear."

Taking a seat beside her, I reached out and clasped her hand, the connection grounding me in the present moment. "I'm here, Mom. I've brought your medication."

As she took a sip of water and swallowed the pills, gratitude crossed her face. "Thank you, sweetheart." Her familiar voice soothed my troubles.

In that tender exchange, I understood the magnitude of the decision I had made. Though the allure of a love left behind in a different time still tugged at my heart, my responsibility to my family remained paramount.

Sitting there beside my mother, I vowed to cherish the memories of Leo, embracing them as a treasure hidden deep within my heart. From now on, I would once again choose to look to the future; I might not be able to go to the Curtis Institute of Music, but I could still make a life worth living where my family was kept close.

Perhaps, in due time, I could become a piano teacher like Mrs. Johnson. I had never considered it before, but I had enjoyed seeing Amelia flourish under my tutelage.

***

Weeks turned into a blur of doctor's appointments, treatments, and hopeful anticipation. Chemotherapy seemed to be yielding positive results for my mother, as evidenced by the doctor's reassuring smile as he displayed the latest scans. The images revealed a shrinking mass, a beacon of hope amidst the darkness of the illness that had threatened to engulf our lives.

My heart swelled, tears pooling in my eyes as my mother's face lit up with a flicker of renewed hope. The uncertainty that had gripped our family began to loosen its hold, replaced by a glimmer of optimism for the future.

Amidst the healing journey my mother embarked upon, a letter arrived, bearing the familiar handwriting of my dear brother, Lyle. With bated breath, we opened the envelope, devouring each word as if it were a lifeline connecting us to the world outside our own.

Lyle's words flowed across the page, infused with the resilience and strength that had always characterized him. He wrote of his experiences, his triumphs, and his challenges, sharing anecdotes that drew a smile to my mother's face and tears of pride to my own eyes. He was doing well, carving out his path, a testament to the indomitable spirit that ran through our family's veins.

As I read the letter aloud, my mother listened, her fingers intertwining with mine. Together, we reveled in the small victories, finding solace in the progress my mother made with each passing day. We celebrated the flickering hope that took root in our hearts, fueling our determination to forge ahead, united in the face of adversity.

I had thrown away the dress from Leo's time and now decided it was time to set aside the green book which had remained my nightly companion, its pages inscribed with my adventures back in time. I pushed the book into the back of my closet and took out my uniform for Grace's Place, the diner I worked at.

I hopped on my bicycle, the cool breeze rustling through my hair as I pedaled my way towards my workplace. The familiar jingle of the bell chimed as I entered the cozy diner, the scent of sizzling bacon and freshly brewed coffee enveloping the air.

I wore a crisp, powder blue uniform adorned with a white apron, a symbol of my role as a waitress at Grace's Place. The uniform clung to me like a second skin, the starched dress and collar making me feel like I had a sense of purpose and professionalism.

The diner itself was the town's haven, with checkerboard linoleum flooring, red vinyl booths that gleamed under the soft lighting, and a long bar lined with chrome stools. The walls were adorned with posters and photographs, capturing the essence of current pop culture. The jukebox in the corner played the latest hits, adding a touch of youthfulness to the bustling atmosphere.

As I made my rounds, I greeted the customers with a warm smile and a friendly 'Good morning!' Taking orders, jotting them down on my notepad, and ensuring everyone's needs were met became second nature to me. The regulars at the bar would banter with me, engaging in lighthearted conversations about the latest news, music, and local gossip.

"Hey there, Rosemary! How about a cup of Joe to start my day?" Frank, a middle-aged gentleman with a mischievous twinkle in his eye, grinned as he held up his empty coffee mug.

"Coming right up, Frank. Extra cream, just the way you like it." I hustled over and poured steaming hot coffee into his cup.

At the booths, families and friends gathered, chatting and sharing stories over plates of fluffy pancakes and sizzling bacon. I juggled multiple orders, skillfully balancing trays filled with mouthwatering dishes, ensuring each one reached its intended destination without a hitch.

As I passed by the counter, I exchanged quick words of camaraderie with the fellow wait staff, a tight-knit group bonded by our shared experiences and long hours spent together. We offered support, lending a hand during busy periods and sharing stories during quieter moments, creating an atmosphere of teamwork and friendship.

"Rosemary, table four needs their check," Maria, a seasoned waitress, called out, her voice carrying a hint of urgency.

"Got it, Maria." I retrieved the check from the register and delivered it to the awaiting customers.

The day at Grace's Place flowed seamlessly, a whirlwind of laughter, conversation, and delicious food. With every satisfied customer and every smile exchanged, I felt a sense of fulfillment.

I wiped the counter with a damp cloth, my eyes scanning the bustling diner as I made mental notes of the orders to be taken. The chime of the door caught my attention, and I glanced up to see a handsome man with wavy brown hair enter the diner. He exuded a certain charm and confidence that immediately drew my notice.

As he walked towards the bar, I flashed him a friendly smile. "Good morning! What can I get you?" I held my pen poised above my notepad.

"Coffee, please." His voice carried a hint of amusement. His eyes met mine, and I couldn't help but notice the spark of mischief within them.

I poured him a steaming cup of coffee, the aroma filling the air between us. "Here you go, one cup of coffee." I reached forward, placing it in front of him.

He leaned against the counter, a playful smile on his lips. "Thanks, Rosemary. I'm Gary Moore, by the way." He continued to smile as he kept his gaze fixed on me.

"Nice to meet you, Gary." My cheeks flushed at his

flirtatious demeanor. I leaned against the counter as well, my curiosity piqued. "So, what brings you to Grace's Place today?"

He chuckled, stirring a spoon in his coffee. "Honestly, I think it was fate. I heard this place had the best coffee in town, and I couldn't resist checking it out for myself. But now that I'm here, I find myself more interested in the lovely company." His eyes lingered on mine.

I laughed, warmth spreading up my cheeks. "Well, I'm flattered, Gary. But I'm working right now, and I should probably keep my attention on the other customers."

Gary's smile widened, and he nodded in understanding. "I respect that, Rosemary. But I hope you'll reconsider joining me for a cup of coffee when you're off duty. I have a feeling we could have some great conversations."

I tilted my head, charmed by his persistence. "You're quite the charmer, aren't you? All right, Gary, I appreciate the offer, but I'll have to decline for now. Maybe another time."

He leaned back, sipping his coffee, determination in his eyes. "Fair enough, Rosemary. I won't push it. But mark my words, I'll be back. And I'll ask you again. Until then, enjoy your day."

I couldn't help but chuckle at his confident yet playful demeanor. "I'll be waiting for that second cup of coffee, Gary. Until then, take care."

As he left the bar, our eyes met one last time, a silent understanding passing between us. I returned to my duties, my mind still buzzing with the unexpected encounter. There was something about Gary Moore's charming persistence that left a lingering impression that reminded me of Leo.

Perhaps our paths would cross again, and who knew what the future might hold?

Afterword

Thank you for reading *Sage, Rosemary, and Time*. Since writing *Rose Through Time*, the first novel in the A Magical Bookshop Novel series, I wanted to give Rosemary her own story. Whether this is your first time reading one of my time travel novels or if you are a returning reader, I appreciate that you took a chance on my books.

If you have the chance, I would love it if you left a review on a platform of your choosing. Reviews are a tremendous help in bringing my novel to new readers and I greatly appreciate them.

Is this your first foray into my A Magical Bookshop Novel series? Keep reading for the first two chapters of *Rose Through Time*. If you'd like to stay up to date on future projects and receive bonus content, sign up for my newsletter on my website.

Happy reading!

Rose Through Time

CHAPTER 1

A Forgotten Piano

Twelve pairs of bright young eyes stared up at me as I told them that a substitute English teacher would take over my classes next week. Well, maybe only ten pairs, as Tommy, a heavily freckled kid with glasses and a penchant for sticky fingers, was exchanging playing cards with his friend and classmate, Noah. A smart but easily distracted boy with piercing green eyes, who often wore Spider-Man t-shirts, and always had to show me his newest comic book.

I stopped talking and leaned against the desk which was cluttered with my students' homework, colored pencils and pens, and a "#1 Teacher" mug I had received as a gift. I scraped my throat until Tommy and Noah stopped their whispering and looked up at me with embarrassment. There were only a few minutes left, so I continued on with what I had to say.

"Now that we are all paying attention, I want you to promise me that you will be nice to Miss Singer who will be your substitute teacher next week. Your writing assignment will still be due on Friday and I will grade it when I return. I hope you all have a wonderful weekend, and I will see you all in a week."

"We'll miss you, Miss Hart," a tall girl with strawberry blonde braids and a small upturned nose chirped from the front row.

"We'll miss you," the other kids joined in as they stood, picked up their backpacks, and filed out of the classroom. I lingered for a moment, taking in the rows of students' desks and askew chairs, the motivational posters on the walls which were my idea to brighten up the room, and a large sheet of paper tacked up next to the white-board featuring impressions of the children's hands in multi-colored puff paint and their own hand scrawled names. My fingers traced the desks as I pushed in the chairs and tidied up the room before leaving.

My black purse started to buzz as I said goodbye to the receptionist. I reached around in its bowels until I pulled out my phone in its bejeweled case. The word "Mom" popped up on the screen in bright letters and I pressed the green button.

"There you are, honey, are you still coming over to help with the preparations? Maybe you can make a stop on the way and bring over more napkins; I'm worried we don't have enough. And since you are going anyways, can you also grab a bag of ice."

There was a local grocery chain near the school, so I swung by there to pick up the groceries. Snatching a shopping basket from the pile by the entrance, I wound my way through the aisles. My mother told me that we needed napkins and ice; so I grabbed those. Then I got myself a candy bar. I felt like I needed something sugary and chocolatey. Using self check-out, I paid for my items and dropped them in the trunk of my car. Once I settled back into the drivers seat, I took a moment for myself. I unwrapped the candy bar and bit into its chewy caramel center, savoring the sweet flavor. Then I stuffed the empty wrapper in my cup-holder, buckled my seat belt, and drove to meet my mom.

I parked my blue Nissan Sentra in the concrete driveway next to my mother's silver SUV and grabbed the napkins and bag of ice from the trunk. I walked up the ocher flagstones lined with smaller decorative stones that formed a path around the cream-colored, stucco, two storied house that used to be my grandmother's home. My fingers trembled and I choked back tears as I remembered how, as a child, I spent many days running around in the backyard in my bathing suit, my grandmother laughing and following me with the water hose until I tired, or how I helped her whip-up extravagant sorbets which we promptly devoured. I would never again see her kind face surrounded by a halo of silver hair, bound back on top of her head as she strained over a crossword puzzle or taste the golden crusted cinnamon apple pie that she baked each fall with crisp apples from her own tree.

I used my shoulder to press open the side door leading into the garage and dropped the heavy bag of ice on top of the freezer box in the corner. I set the napkins on top of the storage shelf holding tins filled with a random array of screws and nails along with clear plastic bins that held a bunch of scarves and other cold weather gear. Then, I popped the top of the freezer which was still stacked with storage containers filled with my grandma's homemade stew and assorted cas-seroles. I moved some containers to the side and plopped in the bag of ice that had started to thaw, leaving the tips of my fingers moist.

"Is that you, honey?" my mom's voice shouted from inside the house.

"Yeah, I just put the ice in the freezer," I replied. My mom opened the door leading from the garage to the kitchen, her hair tied up in a messy ponytail, tendrils of copper hair framing her face like a halo of fire interlaced with shoots of silver. Seeing my mom with bags beneath her eyes spreading out like bruises and her clothing in disarray when she normally was groomed to perfection, brought home my reason for being there. "Mom," my voice hitched; she took one step towards me and enveloped me with her arms.

"I know," she whispered against my ear; her chest sunk as she exhaled deeply. Her hand gripped mine tightly, and she led me further into the house. The air was heavy with the sulfuric scent of eggs and the cloying perfume of the floral bouquets placed throughout the house, making my stomach turn. My mom had prepped her chunky potato salad along with deviled eggs, made special by the finely minced onion and pinch of curry powder she added as her secret ingredients. I moved them from the kitchen island to the fridge which was already stocked with drinks.

"I already cleaned the kitchen, but I could use your help with the other rooms. The nursing home isn't coming until tonight to pick up the equipment," my mom said. The foldable hospital bed my grandmother had spent her last days on stood stripped of its linen in the corner of the living room together with an empty IV pole, the only clinical distraction from the otherwise cozy but old-fashioned room. My grandmother had been fond of doilies, and she had them draped over every possible flat surface, including the big boxed TV that still worked. On the side table, next to the brown leather love seat, my mom had placed a poster-sized black and white portrait of my grandmother when she was younger. She stared straight at the camera with a smile that said she had a secret. Her hair was coiled up and fastened with a clip, wearing a white blouse and pearl earrings, the same earrings that now made their home in my jewelry box after she gave them to me for my eighteenth birthday.

"You look so much like her," my mom said. "She was about twenty-five in this picture, the same age you are now. I'm glad you got her chestnut curls and green almond shaped eyes instead of the reddish hair your late grandfather gave me."

"I miss her," I said.

"Me too, but I don't believe she's gone. She'll be here looking over us and I want to make sure she'll be proud of the reception tomorrow," she said patting my cheek. "I'll go outside to set up the tables."

My mom slid open the French doors and went into the backyard. I fetched the old Hoover vacuum and ran it over the carpet to make sure the floor was clean and fluffy. My grandmother was never satisfied until her beige carpet had straight streaks vacuumed into it. I glanced around the room again, taking in the wedding and family pictures framed on the wall behind the love seat, porcelain knickknacks on the heavy mahogany cupboard, and the Bavarian cuckoo clock hanging on the other wall above the stereo system that still played tapes, then I placed the vacuum back into the utility closet and joined my mom outside. She had started to set up the party tables; I helped her fold out the last one and set out the plastic chairs. It wasn't supposed to be windy today and tomorrow so we set up one of those pop-up shades but fastened it with ground-stakes just in case. Thankfully, May wasn't scorching hot yet, so we could host outside, otherwise my grandmother's house would have gotten cramped.

"Will you wait for the nursing home people to pick up the bed? I've got to go home and get your dad some dinner and lay my things out for tomorrow. Your dress is already ironed and hanging in your old room. You are staying with us tonight, right? That way we can drive together tomorrow morning," my mom asked.

"Yes, I'll be there as soon as the bed's picked up. Save me a plate," I said and walked her to the front door. She took her purse from the wooden coat rack on the left side of the door and fished out the car keys. I waved her goodbye as she reversed into the street and took off in the silver SUV. Once my mom left, the house turned extremely quiet and reverent, almost like a tomb. I shook that thought away. This was my grandmother's house, and besides her last days, it was filled with good memories. I took a seat on the bench in front of my grandmother's piano and opened the lid to reveal the black and white keys. I remembered her sitting at it with a straight back and her head held high while she played; it would be sad to see the instrument go but I didn't have the space and my mom never really learned to play, much to my grandmother's discontent. The piano beckoned me so I slid my fingers across the smooth keys, testing their sound, and then I couldn't help but play one of my grandmother's favorite songs. An hour later, around seven o'clock, the doorbell finally rang. I brushed my skirt as I stood, closed the lid to the piano, and went to answer the door.

"Hi, so sorry for your loss, ma'am. We're here to pick up the bed and IV pole," a young man, probably in his early twenties, with a Hillsbrook nursing home tag clipped to his blue polo said. I nodded and told him and his partner, a bigger middle-aged woman wearing a colorful scrub top, to follow me into the living room. There, the man started wheeling out the bed while the woman squeezed my arm sympathetically. She was holding a pen and some papers in her hand.

"I just need you to sign some paperwork while Ben loads up the van, okay?" she said with a warm tone. I nodded as she pointed at the sections I needed to put my signature on. Ben folded up the hospital bed then rolled it over the freshly vacuumed carpet and out the door. Now I'd have to vacuum the streaks back in, I thought, as I signed the paperwork. The woman was kind and didn't rush me, but her gentle concern didn't feel authentic. Instead, it felt performative. It wasn't her fault. She probably had to deal with bereaved family members all the time. It didn't take long for Ben to finish loading. The Hillsbrook employees and medical equipment being gone from the house made a huge difference. The living room looked like a living room again and not like a glorified hospital room. Without the clinical reminder, it looked almost as if my grandmother could walk in again and sit down to watch her soap operas. I redid the vacuumed lines in the carpet and put away the old Hoover. Then, I straightened the decorative pillows scattered on the chair and sofa, walked out of the house with purpose, and locked the front door behind me.

CHAPTER 2

A Family Gathering

I shimmied into the black cocktail dress my mom left hanging on my wardrobe door. She deftly coiled my hair up into a French twist while I applied waterproof mascara and dabbed on fuchsia lip stain.

"You look beautiful," she said as she brushed my cheek. "I'm going to finish up the last touches on myself, and I'll see you downstairs. Your dad is already waiting by the door, so we can leave in fifteen minutes."

My stomach filled with nerves as I stared at myself in the vanity mirror, the edges still covered in pictures from high school. Most of the pictures were of me and my friend Nicole; us in full glam at our prom, holding s'mores by a campfire during a camping trip with my parents, at fourteen dressed in matching bikinis at the pool. My favorite was the picture my mom took of us at the school talent show. We'd dressed up in matching sparkly leotards and performed a dance routine. I still cringed at the dance moves that were so corny. Nicole and I didn't realize this at the time, bless our teenage brains, but now every time we talked about it we were in hysterics. My mom still had a tape of the whole talent show in her media cabinet.

My eyes drifted to my jewelry box; my grandmother's pearl earrings prominently displayed. I picked them up and decided to wear them. My fingers shook a bit, but I stretched them a couple of times, stood, brushed invisible lint from my dress, and joined my parents downstairs.

"Oh, I forgot to tell you that the Realtor called about the house. I'm sorry I can't take any extra time off from work. Are you sure you still want to go through and pack up your grandmother's things this week to get the house ready for selling?" my mom asked. "I hate that I'm asking you to do this, but the idea of a stranger combing through the house to pack up all my mother's belongings just gives me the shivers. I want her things to be handled by someone she loved."

"Of course, Mom. I know it is important to you."

"If you find anything of your grandmother's that you like, please take it; I know she'd want you to have it."

"I'll sort through the sentimental items for anything you might like to go through at a later time together with Dad," I promised my mom.

"Thanks, sweetie."

My dad handed my mom her purse and held open the door for us. We shuffled into his white sedan, and he drove us towards the Sunny Acres Funeral Home and Cemetery. Parking in the large gravel parking lot, I could almost imagine we were going to a nice park, if not for the headstones lining the plots. Artificially watered, bright green grass covered the ground and palm trees lined the cemetery, belying an oasis in the middle of the desert climate.

It was a nice service, in how far a funeral can be nice. The priest covered my grandmother's life, reciting the highlights we had fed him. His deep voice comforted us as he relayed how my grandmother had worked as waitress at a local breakfast place before she became a piano teacher, where my grandfather, Gary Moore, had taken a shining to her. Every day, he returned to order two cups of coffee, then he would ask her to join him. After a month of declining his offer, she finally accepted and joined him for a cup after her shift ended. They were married forty-one years, and raised my mother, Holly Moore-Hart, together, when he died of a stroke in 2011. My grandmother was lost for a long time after his death, but thankfully she had found close friends in the ladies from her bingo group and gardening club. The three bingo club ladies— Patty, Wanda, and Shirley— stood together with us to pay their respects. Michael Jones, a gardening club member, had also joined the service. I was touched at seeing my grandmother's friends and our extended family all together to celebrate her life. My mom had picked out the wedding picture that stood displayed on a stand by the pastor's mike. Underneath the photo, it stated my grandmother's name along with her birth and death dates: Rosemary Scott-Moore, 1949-2020.

We all filed into each other's respective cars once the service was over, with my dad's car going first to lead the procession to my grandmother's house.

"That was beautiful, I think. Don't you agree? I'm glad her friends showed up; I invited them to join us at the reception," my mom said as she fidgeted with her fingernails.

"It was very respectful, Holly," my dad said. "We made it through the service, and we will make it through the reception. Just remember we are all here to reminisce and celebrate your mother's life; you can take it easy. Everyone will understand if you don't serve them; the reception is potluck style anyway."

"Yeah, Mom, I think Grandma would have been proud of the service, to see her friends and family all gathered together. I'll take charge of accepting and setting out all the food so you can just grab a drink for yourself and talk to the rest of the family," I said as I squeezed her shoulder. My dad parked in the driveway and the other guests following us parked on the side of the road. I let my parents go inside first to give them a breather as I stood at attention by the front door to greet everyone and thank them for their food.

My cousin on my dad's side, Sofia Hart-Brooks, arrived first with her husband, Joshua. They handed me a potato casserole. Followed by her brother Ryan and his girlfriend Amber with green beans. Next, I greeted my Aunt Paula and Uncle Robert. They brought a container of salmon roll ups made with spinach tortillas and a fruit salad heavy with whipped topping and pistachio Jello mix. I told them to set out on the kitchen island next to the paper plates, napkins, and cutlery.

My second cousin on my mom's side, Eric Scott, hugged me and expressed his condolences. He and his boyfriend, Thomas, brought a vegetable platter with carrot, celery, and bell pepper with a ranch dip.

I let in a stream of other family members and close friends, which included Jason Scott and his girlfriend, Lauren. Most guests had already arrived when I welcomed my grandmother's brother, Lyle, and his wife, Terry. Finally, Nicole Moreno, my best friend since high school, showed up to give me emotional support. My grandmother's friends from the bingo group and gardening club arrived last. Patty Decarlo dropped a pan of lasagna in my hands. After closing the front door behind me, I took it to set out with the rest of the food. Everyone had come together and helped create a bountiful spread of food. Besides my mom's deviled eggs and potato salad, there were buttery dinner rolls, a cheesy and crispy potato casserole that made my mouth water, and a green bean casserole covered in fried onions. My aunt Donna baked a smooth and creamy cheesecake.

My mom thanked everyone for coming and loaded up her first paper plate with a scoop of Patty's lasagna, two of her own deviled eggs, and a dinner roll. Once she stepped away to sit down at the table in the backyard, the rest of the guests loaded up their plates and joined her. I waited until everyone else had served themselves before I took a moment for myself, slowly picking out the foods I wanted to try. Concern for my mother made me take care of all the greeting, but keeping up appearances was hard. The muscles around my lips were already strained from trying to keep a smile plastered on my face. With the back of my hand, I wiped away a tear sneaking down my cheek, careful to not mess up my make-up. I let out a sigh and started piling my plate with potato casserole and Patty's lasagna which scented the air with crusty Parmesan, savory beef, and tomatoes. For good measure, I also dropped a few carrots from Eric's vegetable platter on my plate. Just because it was funeral reception, didn't mean I shouldn't try to add something healthy.

My mom was listening to Lyle talk about his sister, my grandmother, when I dropped my plate on the table and sat down next to her. Terry, Lyle's wife, took a big bite of potato salad, wiped her mouth, and turned her attention to me. "Where is Michael? He's such a handsome young man. You are such a beautiful couple together; I can only imagine the cute babies you'll have," she said. I blanched and a hush fell around me. I mentally thanked my friend who came to my rescue, so I didn't have to answer.

"Michael ended up being someone who didn't deserve Rose, so they broke up. Serves him right in my opinion," Nicole said.

"You are right, Nicole, but Rose isn't getting younger," Terry continued. "You should really get back into the saddle and meet a new man," she said pointedly at me.

"I am content with being on my own for now," I said. "Please excuse me, I'm going to fetch another drink." I pushed out my chair and marched to the kitchen while my mom looked embarrassed; Nicole followed me on my heels.

"Don't listen to her. She still thinks it's 1940 and you need a man to provide for you so you can just pop out babies and medicate yourself with laudanum." She patted my arm and continued, "Let's just sit here for a moment so you can take a breather and eat some of this cheesecake." She pulled out a chair for me, which I took, then sat down opposite me. "So, how are you really?"

I sliced us both a share of the cheesecake and handed her one of them on a paper plate. I poked at the creamy and tangy filling until it turned to crumbs before answering. "Honestly, I'm not sure. Between my grandmother dying and Michael breaking up with me, I don't know what to feel. Did you know he told me I was boring?"

"You aren't boring. He was just being rude."

"No, I am though. With everything, I play it safe. Why can't I just let go and live a little. He wanted to have someone to explore the world with, and he found that in someone that was not me. Can't even say I blame him. I'm hurt that he cheated, but I don't think I loved him. He was just a safe choice and it was better to stay with what was familiar than to dive back into the deep end. I don't want to end up filled with regrets; maybe something adventurous could still happen to me," I said, followed by a bite of dessert.

"I think you just need to turn your brain off and stop worrying sometime. We are young, and we'll get where we need to go. There's no need to be in a rush to get to some arbitrary finish line which we've been told we should wanna reach."

"Maybe you're right," I said with a sigh.

"Damn straight," Nicole said. "You know me, I'm always right."

"Unless you are wrong," I said with a wink.

"Ah, but that never happens." Nicole scooped some cheesecake into her mouth and licked her lips. "I think we should have a girls' night."

"We should. I'll be pretty busy packing up my grandmother's home, but we should hang out soon. We never get together as often as we used to."

One of the bingo ladies entered the kitchen. "Where is your bathroom," she said.

"Down the hall and on your right," I said pointing in the direction of the front door.

"Thanks," she said, then before leaving the kitchen she added, "I am so sorry for your loss. Your grandmother was a lovely woman."

"Thank you, I appreciate it," I said.

"It really was a lovely service, very dignified. I think

Rosemary would have been proud." Nicole squeezed my hand when the woman left.

"Just a little longer and then you'll be able to rest. Promise me though, that if you need to talk for any reason at all, you will call me." I nodded. "I mean it. I am here, always."

"Thank you for coming, for being here for me," I said, returning the squeeze of her hand.

Acknowledgments

If you've made it this far, I want to give a big thank you to everyone who has helped me publish this book. Seriously, I couldn't do it without your assistance, guidance, and support. It truly means the world to me. When I first dreamed of being an author, I never imagined I would have this many people excited about the words I furiously scribbled down on paper. It was strange writing this prequel. While I loved lingering in the 60s and exploring the 18th century, it truly felt like finishing a chapter of my life.

With the prequel to my A Magical Bookshop Novel series done and in the hands of readers, I'm ready to continue writing new stories in different genres. I want to thank my family for always liking and sharing my posts and my beta readers for taking the time to read the unpolished versions.

I hope you'll continue. There aren't enough words to describe how grateful I am for all the support, kindness, and much-needed error-catching.

I also want to give a shoutout to my editor, Megan Sanders, who has been along for the ride since my first novel, Rose Through Time, back in 2021. And Patterson Photography for my beautiful author photos. Last but not least, I want to thank you for reading because without you I wouldn't be doing what I love.

May we meet again in the next book!

About The Author

Harmke Buursma is a writer, and author of the novel Rose Through Time. She uses her background in Journalism to help bring her fictional characters and worlds to life. When she isn't writing, she likes to read as many books as she can get her hands on. Originally born and raised in The Netherlands, Harmke now lives in Las Vegas with her husband Matthew and two dogs.

Harmke Buursma
Photo by Patterson Photography

For more information about Harmke and her books, visit www.harmkebuursma.com.

Books By This Author

ROSE THROUGH TIME

WILLIAM THROUGH TIME

BETH THROUGH TIME

ANNE THROUGH TIME

SAGE, ROSEMARY, AND TIME

Audiobooks

Rose Through Time now also available as an audiobook narrated by Krista Nicely

Rediscover the magic of the first installment of the A Magical Bookshop Novel series now available on Amazon, Audible, and Itunes.

For more information, check out www.harmkebuursma.com

9 781962 506960